# Creatures

## Atishoo! Atishoo!
## All Fall Down!

Turning away from the cage, Kel started to walk towards the door. The others followed.

And Chocky said, quite clearly, "Susie won't hurt *you*."

They all stopped dead. Turned. Stared. Birds can't grin, but if Chocky had been human there would have been a smirk on his face.

"Susie won't hurt *you*," he repeated, then paused as if he was thinking – or listening to something no one else could hear. "Susie *likes* you."

**Look for other Creatures titles
by Louise Cooper:**

# Creatures

## Atishoo! Atishoo!
## All Fall Down!

## Louise Cooper

For my mother, Pat, who gave me the ideas for some of Chocky's favourite sayings. You know which ones!

Scholastic Children's Books
Commonwealth House, 1–19 New Oxford Street,
London WC1A 1NU, UK
London ~ New York ~ Toronto ~ Sydney ~ Auckland
Mexico City ~ New Delhi ~ Hong Kong
First published by Scholastic Ltd, 1999

ISBN 0 590 63770 3

All rights reserved
Typeset by Falcon Oast Graphic Art
Printed by Cox & Wyman Ltd, Reading, Berks

10 9 8 7 6 5 4 3 2 1

# 1

"Chocky's quiet, isn't he?" said Steve.

"I know," Kelvin agreed. "He hasn't said a word all morning. That's not like him at all."

"What's up with him, d'you think?"

Kelvin shrugged. "Dunno. Maybe he doesn't like the smell of the paint. Can't say I blame him."

He peered more closely at the large cage that stood on the table at the side of the classroom, then wiggled a finger through the bars. But Chocky, the mynah bird, only shuffled along his perch, put his head on one side and stared back with beady, orange-rimmed eyes.

"Come on, Chocky," Kelvin cajoled. "Say something! *Here we go, here we go, here we go—*"

"Oh, shut up, Kel!" Kate Ransome, who was in the same year as the two boys, had moved up behind them and was hovering. "He knows better things than football chants! Anyway, you shouldn't be encouraging him. If he starts talking, Mrs Dwyer will only make us take him out."

As if conjured up by her words, their class teacher came in at that moment. Kate mooched over to her desk, and Kelvin and Steve reluctantly followed. The general classroom chatter dropped to a mumble as Mrs Dwyer sat down.

"Good morning, everyone." Her nose wrinkled.

"Morning, Mrs D." "Morning." "Yeah." "Mmm." There was a vague chorus of responses. Mrs Dwyer sighed, but didn't make her usual comments about speaking up and remembering manners. Instead, she looked at Chocky in his cage and said, "Will someone kindly tell me why that bird is in here, and not in the new activity room?"

"He can't stay in there, Mrs Dwyer," Kate said earnestly. "It's all the paint – we thought it might make him ill."

Mrs Dwyer looked hard at her, obviously suspecting a ruse. But Kate's expression was perfectly innocent, and at last she said, "Well . . . I suppose he can stay until the smell fades. It's bad enough in the rest of the school, so what it must be like in the new block. . . Just as long as he keeps quiet."

"I'm sure he will, Mrs Dwyer," said Kate sweetly.

"All right, Kate, there's no need to overdo it." Mrs D's nose twitched again, and she sniffed. "This paint smell *is* a nuisance, but we'll just have to put up with it until—" The words collapsed suddenly into a sneeze. Immediately, from his cage, Chocky mimicked loudly, "A-TISH-oo!"

Mrs Dwyer glared at Chocky, and as the fit of giggles round the classroom subsided she said, "When I said quiet, Kate, I *meant* quiet!"

"Sorry," said Kate, and Kel, who was sitting nearest to the cage, banged the bars and added, "Shut up, Chocky!"

"Atishoo!" Chocky remarked again. Then he ruffled his feathers, turned his back and appeared to go to sleep.

"Good," said Mrs Dwyer. "Now, let's hope the silence lasts."

It did, for a while. But Mrs Dwyer suffered from hay fever and the fresh-paint smell irritated her nose. She kept sneezing – and every time she did, Chocky gleefully echoed the noise. Then, of course, the jokers in the class started pretending to sneeze, just for the fun of making Chocky do it again, and at last Mrs D's patience snapped. Chocky had to go – smell or no smell. Two of them could take him back to the activity room, right *now*.

Kel grabbed one side of the cage before anyone else could even move, and Steve beat Kate to it by a hair's-breadth. Between them they lugged the cage out of the classroom and set off along the corridor.

"A-TISH-oo!" said Chocky.

"Yeah, and Atishoo to you too!" Kel told him. "It's your own fault, you dumb bird."

"Never mind," said Steve. "It gets us out of class for a few minutes, doesn't it?"

They headed for the new block of the

4

school, which had only been finished a few weeks ago, just before the summer term began. It had replaced a jumble of old 1940s prefabs, which in their turn had been put up after the original Victorian schoolhouse was hit by a bomb during the Second World War. There were six new classrooms, an assembly hall and, through a set of glass doors and down a long corridor, a state-of-the-art science lab. And of course the activity room. "Activity" seemed to be an official cover-up name for stuff that didn't have anywhere else to go, and the room was a mish-mash of everything from surplus art materials to the school's wildlife collection and the little kids' pets corner.

In two weeks from next Saturday there was going to be a grand opening ceremony for the block; parents and governors had all been invited and the local mayor was going to unveil a plaque in the hall. Kel couldn't see what the fuss was all about – it was only a building, after all – but opening day would probably be a laugh if nothing else.

Chocky had gone quiet again as they carried him along the corridor. He was sidling up and down his perch, eyeing the clean new walls to either side. Then, as the boys put the cage down outside the activity room and Steve went to open the door, the mynah bird said suddenly, "Susie's here!"

"Huh?" Kel and Steve both looked at the cage in surprise.

"What a weird voice," said Steve. "I've never heard him do that one before, have you?"

Kel hadn't. Chocky was an excellent mimic, and if you ignored the fact that what he said sounded as if it was coming down a crackly 'phone line, he could do passable impersonations of half the class and a few teachers into the bargain. This voice, though, was something completely new. Squeaky and a bit googoo, like someone imitating a little kid.

"What did he say?" Steve asked. "I didn't hear it properly."

As if he had understood, Chocky waggled his tail feathers and said again: "Susie's here!"

"I don't know any Susies in the school, do you?" said Kel.

"No. Not any Sues or Susans, either." Steve grinned. "Maybe one of the teachers has been giving him secret lessons." He put his face against the cage and pulled a face. "Who's

Susie, then, Chocky? Eh? Who's Susie?"

Chocky squawked. "Susie says, atishoo!" he announced. "Atishoo, atishoo!"

"Come on, Steve, stop mucking around." Kel nudged his friend. "We'd better get back before Mrs D works out how long we're taking."

Chocky didn't say anything else as they carried him into the activity room and put him in his usual place at the far end, between the goldfish and the stick insects. The smell of paint wasn't too bad, and with a last, "OK, Chocky? See you, then," the boys left.

Chocky fixed a beady eye on the door as it shut behind them. "Chocky biscuit?" he said hopefully. It was his favourite treat, and the reason behind his name. But there was no one to give him a piece of biscuit, and after a minute he stopped staring at the door and hopped round to face the wall.

"A-TISH-oo," he announced to himself.

There was something strange in the way he said it. Strange, and not very pleasant at all. . .

# 2

In some ways it was great having a mynah bird for a school pet. But in others – such as when his cage needed cleaning out – it was no fun at all. And this morning, the cage-cleaning was Kel's job.

It was break time, and everyone else was outside enjoying the warm weather and sunshine. Kel should have come in early and done his task before lessons began. But yesterday he'd borrowed a computer game from someone, and stayed awake secretly playing it long after Mum and Dad had gone to bed. So he couldn't wake up properly this morning, and he'd got to school late . . . and so on. Now he was grumpily changing liner trays and emptying dishes, casting wistful glances towards the windows, while Chocky sat on one end of his perch and watched with what looked, to Kel, like a mischievous spark in his eyes.

"You peck me," Kel warned him, "you even *think* about it, and I'll feed you to the nearest cat!"

Chocky flexed first one foot, then the other, and said, "Come on, you Re-e-e-eds! Chocky biscuit?"

Despite his mood, Kel grinned. "Later. Anyway, you never finished the last one; there's crumbs everywhere." In a burst of energy he attacked the cage floor with his brush. "You're the messiest bird ever hatched, you know that?"

Chocky said a rude word.

"Yeah, and I got the blame for teaching you that, and it wasn't me!" He still owed Steve for that one, Kel reminded himself.

Still, having Chocky around certainly made school a lot less boring. Quite how they *had* got him was a bit of a tangled tale. He'd belonged to the Deputy Head's wife's brother or cousin or something, and when the brother/ cousin/something had suddenly decided to emigrate, he'd dumped Chocky on his unsuspecting relatives. Mrs Deputy Head was allergic to feathers and couldn't have a bird in the house, so Chocky had come to join the menagerie of school pets. Now he spent term time at the school, and in the holidays there were always plenty of volunteers willing to take him home. Steve had volunteered for the last Christmas holidays, and in the space of two weeks he and Kel had taught Chocky a lot. *Too* much, according to Kate, but Kate could be very prissy when it suited her, and she was probably just jealous.

Anyway, Chocky had a lot of friends, and he never went short of attention. Like that time last term, Kel remembered, when one of the Year Fours had let him out of his cage. He cackled to himself, recalling the mayhem as everyone from the Head downwards had turned the school upside-down trying to catch Chocky, who was equally determined not to be caught. They'd finally lured him with the inevitable chocolate biscuit, but not before he'd caused havoc. Maybe, Kel thought, there was some scope there for a bit of fun at the new block's grand opening? If someone just happened to forget to lock the cage door again. . .

"Time to go home!" announced Chocky. "T.G.I.F.!"

"Yeah, well, it's not Friday, and it's still morning," Kel told him. "Come on, you over-grown budgie, shift up and let me put your food and water back. . ." He reached into the cage with the dishes, keeping a wary eye on Chocky's orange beak. He didn't really peck, but he could get a bit playful sometimes.

"There you go." Kel withdrew his hand, unscathed. "All finished."

"Mary-Mary-quite-contrary!" Chocky announced. It was that goo-goo little-kid voice again. Kel pulled a face. Nursery rhymes. Oh, great. The reception class kids must have been getting in here.

"You can do better than that!" he said. "Come on: *Here we go, here we go, here we go!*"

Chocky bounced on his perch. "MaryMary. MaryMary." Then he squawked loudly and added in a rush, "Mary-Brown-went-to-town-with-her-bloomers-hanging-down!"

"Huh?" Kel stared at the bird in astonishment. He'd never heard *that* one before! Where the heck had Chocky got it from?

"Hey, Chocky!" He waggled his fingers outside the bars. "Who taught you that, eh?"

Chocky whistled cheekily, then said: "A-TISH-oo!"

The door banged and Kel looked round to see Kate coming in. "Haven't you finished yet?" she said. "Break's nearly over."

"You don't need to tell me!"

"Well, if you'd got in early instead of—"

"Oh, shut up! Hey, listen, Chocky's learned a new rhyme." Kel turned back to the cage. "Come on, Chocky, say it again. 'Mary Brown went to town. . .'"

Chocky stared at them both in silence.

"Come *on*!" Kel coaxed. "Mary Brown! What did Mary Brown do?"

"Not much, by the sound of it," said Kate sarcastically, when Chocky continued to stare beadily at them. "Fascinating stuff, Kel. Look, are you coming or not? You promised to lend me that book about vampires, and I want to get it now so I can read it in maths class."

"Oh, all right." Kel straightened up. "You

know what your best subject is, don't you, Kate? Nagging. You should take a GCSE in it; you'd get an A."

She pulled a face at him, and with a last glance at Chocky he followed her towards the door.

As they reached it, Chocky said: "Susie's here."

Kate paused and looked back. "What did he say then?"

"Oh, that. He did it yesterday, when Steve and I brought him in here. And in that silly voice, too."

"I don't know any Susies in the school."

"That's what we said."

"Atishoo!" Chocky remarked. Kel and Kate looked at him for a few moments more. Then Kate shrugged, and they went out.

"Susie's here," repeated Chocky. "Susie says, atishoo! Atishoo, atishoo, atishoo!"

And he laughed a strange, gurgling laugh.

It was just typical, Kel thought, that as soon as the irritating smell of the new paint wore off, a cold started to go round the school. By the beginning of the following week half his class had it; every morning there was a pile of excuse notes on Mrs Dwyer's desk, and even those who couldn't persuade parents that they were on their death bed were thick-headed and snuffling.

Kel, of course, didn't catch it. He was furious. He could really have done with a few lazy days in his bedroom, with games and the TV to cheer him up. Steve, with the luck he always seemed to have, was off school. Kate had the cold, too, but she was being a martyr about it, coming in as usual and drooping through classes like a tragic heroine.

The only consolation was that Chocky was back in the classroom. Apparently the decorators had more work to do on the activity room, so all the pets were moved out. Mrs Dwyer was another victim of the cold, and Ms Shipton, her stand-in who also taught English, was vaguer (as someone put it) than a blob of water, so it had been easy to persuade her to have Chocky's cage on a spare desk.

Chocky was soon having the time of his life. It was all the sneezing that did it. With the cold on top of the new paint, just about everyone in the classroom was doing it, and every time they did, Chocky exuberantly copied them. Soon the room was echoing with resounding "A-TISH-oo"s. But there was more to it than that.

Kate was the first one Chocky did it to. Kel, who was sitting near her, saw it coming; Kate shut her eyes, screwed up her face, tried to hold her breath – then grabbed a Kleenex just in time as a gargantuan sneeze exploded echoingly through the room.

"A-TISH-oo!" squawked Chocky. "Susie says, atishoo! Susie says, bless you!"

Ms Shipton put on her harassed look. "Oh, dear, that *bird*!" she said helplessly. "Kate, are you sure you don't want to go home?"

"Yes, thag you, Miz Shibton," Kate snuffled. "I'b all ride, hodestly." She blew her nose.

"Bless you!" Chocky repeated. "Susie says, bless you!"

"Susie" again . . . Kel frowned in puzzlement. Where *had* Chocky learned that? And who was Susie? He thought about it for the rest of the day, but didn't come up with any answers. Then, the next morning, Chocky's mimicry changed. He was still saying "Atishoo!" whenever someone sneezed, but now it was always preceded by "Susie says. . ."

15

Even Ms Shipton started to notice. And when, in the wake of another explosion from Kate, Chocky announced, "Susie says, bless you, bless you!" Ms Shipton sighed heavily, looked around at the class and said,

"Is there *anyone* called Susie in this year?"

"No, Ms Shipton," said Kel. "No one at all."

"Oh. Well, whichever year Susie *is* in, will one of you please tell her to stop encouraging the bird. It's getting on my nerves!"

Someone sniggered, and stifled it. Kel caught Kate's eye and raised his eyebrows, but Kate only shook her head. She was as baffled as he was.

They both hung around in the classroom when school ended for the day. Chocky had to be fed and settled for the night, and Kate offered to help. Kel was glad of it. For one thing it gave him a chance to catch her cold – and for another, he had something to say.

"I know it sounds daft," he confided as they were measuring out Chocky's food ration, "but I think there's something weird about this Susie thing."

Kate sifted sunflower seeds through her fingers. "I agree," she said. "It's as if sub-one's been cubbing id – oh blast, 'scuse be–" She blew her nose forcibly. "As if someone's been coming in when we're not aroud. Around. Oh, I *hate* colds!"

"Swop you," Kel said with feeling.

"You're welcob!" Another snort. "What I was *saying* was, as if someone we don't know's been coming in secredly and teaching Chocky new thigs."

"Yeah. But who?"

"I don't doe." Kate sneezed yet again and Chocky squawked, "A-TISH-oo!"

"Hmm. No Susie that time." Kel bent over the cage. "Hey, Chocky? Where's Susie, Chocky? What does Susie say?"

It was Kel's bad luck that Ms Shipton chose that very moment to come back into the room looking for her jacket, which she'd left behind. She was in time to hear the words "What does Susie say?" and jumped immediately to the wrong conclusion.

"Oh, so it's you two behind this, is it?" It wasn't at all like Ms Shipton to be angry, but for once she had had enough. Striding across the floor, she positioned herself between Kel and the cage and glared at him. "I suppose you think it's funny, do you, Kelvin? Well, it isn't! And Kate – I'd have thought *you'd* know better than to be so silly! Now, I'll tell you both once and once only – if you encourage this bird *any* more, then it goes out of the classroom and it *stays* out! Is that understood?"

Kel and Kate were so astonished that they could only gape at her. After a moment Kate started to say, "Bud we didn'd—" but Ms Shipton wasn't interested.

"You heard me!" she said. "Now, finish what you're doing and go home, the pair of you! I'll wait outside, and if you're not out of this building in five minutes, you'll be in trouble!"

They continued to gape as she stomped out of the classroom, the door slamming behind her. Then Kel broke the silence.

"Strewth. . ." It was an expression he'd picked up from his dad.

"Yeah. . ." said Kate.

Chocky made a funny little crooning noise. He opened his wings and flapped them. Then he turned round, looked very hard at the door through which Ms Shipton had disappeared, and said: "Susie doesn't like you."

They looked at each other. "What did he say. . .?" asked Kel.

As if he'd understood, Chocky repeated, "Susie doesn't *like* you." There was a funny, sing-song tone to the words. And a not very pleasant emphasis.

"Susie says. . ." He crooned again and blinked. Then, so suddenly and startlingly that Kel and Kate both jumped, he shrilled: *"You'll be sorry, you'll be sorry! Susie says, you'll be sorry!"*

"Chocky!" Kel grabbed the cage bars. "Hey, Chocky, stop it, calm down! It's only—"

He didn't get any further. From outside the classroom, somewhere along the corridor, came a noise: a thump, the crunch of breaking glass – and a cry of pain.

It was, unmistakably, Ms Shipton's voice.

# 3

"I didn't even *see* it. . ." Ms Shipton sat on the floor against the corridor wall, holding her hands over her forehead and nose. Blood was dripping between her fingers, and the full-length glass door was cracked and splintered, with small, glittering shards strewn on the floor. "I must have known it was there, but somehow I – I didn't *think*. . ."

The school secretary, two teachers, a gaggle of older pupils and the Head, who had been called from his office, all stared down at her with a mixture of sympathy and dismay.

"Don't worry, love; my car's outside and

we'll soon get you along to the doctor's surgery." The secretary was more practical than anyone else, and she knelt down, trying gently to prise Ms Shipton's hands away and see the damage. "I don't think it's too serious," she added. "Though that glass. . ."

"I don't understand it," said the Head anxiously. "It's toughened; supposed to be unbreakable!"

On the edge of the little crowd, Kel and Kate stood watching the scenario with wide eyes. They didn't say anything, but, just once, they glanced at each other, and each knew what the other was thinking. Chocky's outburst, and Ms Shipton's accident . . . it was a *very* weird coincidence.

Ms Shipton was being helped to her feet. As the secretary shepherded her away, the Head saw Kel and Kate.

"All right, you two, the excitement's over," he said tetchily. "You can go off home."

Kel pointed back. "Just got to give Chocky his food, Mr Wright."

"Well, hurry up about it, then." He set off in the wake of Ms Shipton and the secretary, and Kel and Kate ran back to the classroom.

Chocky greeted them with a whistle. He looked completely innocent.

"He couldn'd have *bade* it habben, could he?" Kate said.

"Course not," Kel replied firmly. And thought: *Could he. . .?*

"Chocky biscuit?" Chocky enquired.

"He seebs all ride dow," said Kate.

Kel glanced sideways at her and half smiled. "Ms Shipton's going to sound just like you tomorrow."

"Oh, shud ub!" She blew her nose again. "That's better! Look, I want to go home. Let's just leave him, yeah?" She picked up her bag, then paused. "If you ask me, it was Steve."

"What was?"

"All this Susie stuff. Steve had Chocky at his house over the Christmas holidays, didn't he? I bet he taught it to him, to wind everyone up."

"That was the holiday before last, though," said Kel. "Jackie Hughes had him at Easter."

"Jackie wouldn't have done it. She hasn't got the brains," Kate said firmly. "No; I bet you anything it was Steve."

It *was* just the sort of thing Steve would do, thought Kel. As for Ms Shipton's accident –

well, it was just a coincidence, wasn't it? Had to be.

"I'll ring Steve tonight," he said. "If he *did* do it, I'll make him tell me."

"Hmm, well, you can try." Kate sounded sceptical. "Oh, rats! My doze – nose – is starding again . . . I'm going. See you toborrow, Choggy."

Chocky watched them as they left the classroom. He whistled again, once. Then he hunched down comfortably on his perch and went to sleep.

Steve was so insistent that he hadn't taught Chocky the Susie routine that Kel believed him. As Steve pointed out, he'd been as puzzled as Kel when Chocky first came out with it. That was true, Kel recalled. It could have been an act, of course, but Steve couldn't act to save his life.

"Anyway," Steve said gloomily, "I'll be back at school tomorrow, so if he does it again I'll see for myself." He cackled suddenly. "Wish I'd been there when the Shipwreck collided with that door!"

"Yeah, well, it wasn't *that* funny," said Kel.

"And it was a bit weird, after what Chocky'd just said."

"Oh, come on! You're not trying to say Chocky put a spell on her or something?" Steve teased.

"No, course not! It was just – I dunno. Strange."

"Just what she deserved, if you ask me," said Steve. "Anyway, I've got to go. See you."

"Yeah. See you."

Kel put the receiver down and stood chewing his lower lip, as he always did when he was thinking. *Susie doesn't like you*, Chocky had said. Then: *Susie says, you'll be sorry*. And seconds later Ms Shipton had walked smack into the door.

*Nah*, he thought, *you're being daft, Kel*. Steve was right: it couldn't possibly have had anything to do with Chocky. Relaxing, he cheered himself up with the reminder that Steve would be back tomorrow. With any luck he'd still be infectious, and Kel might catch the cold at last.

Crossing his fingers, Kel turned and went into the kitchen to find something to eat.

\* \* \*

To Kel and Kate's surprise, Ms Shipton was in school the next morning, sporting an Elastoplast above one eyebrow and a badly bruised nose. Everyone else wanted to know what had happened, but Ms Shipton only mumbled something about an accident and wouldn't go into details. At the back of the classroom, Chocky shuffled around in his cage. He was very quiet, but Kel had the feeling that he was taking an unusually keen interest in all that went on.

Then someone sneezed, and the mynah bird's head came up sharply.

"Susie says, atishoo! Susie says, bless you!"

Ms Shipton gave Kel a glare, which he returned with a helpless, it-wasn't-me-honest shrug. He could feel Steve looking at him but didn't turn round.

English was the first lesson, and eventually everyone settled down to work. There was a bit of a diversion when Kate couldn't find her rollerball pen – quite an expensive one, which she said had definitely been in her bag yesterday afternoon but now appeared to have walked. Ms Shipton, who wasn't in the best of moods to start with, grew edgier and edgier at the fuss, until finally she declared that Kate would just have to use something else – a piece of stick dipped in blood, for all she cared – and look for the wretched pen later.

Huffily, Kate switched to a biro, and peace reigned for a while. They were all writing – or trying to write – a poem on the theme of wildlife. Kel was doing a comic one, which he was quite pleased with; he was bent over his page, concentrating, when out of nowhere an odd little nagging feeling made him look up at Chocky's cage.

Chocky was sitting very still on his perch, watching something intently. Following the direction of his gaze, Kel saw that he was staring at Glenda Parsons, whose desk was in the next row to Kel's. Few people liked Glenda and even fewer trusted her; she was arrogant and rude, and seemed to enjoy going out of her way to be unpleasant whenever she could. Why was Chocky suddenly so interested in her? Kel wondered.

Then he saw that Chocky wasn't looking at Glenda herself, but at the pen in her hand.

The pen looked exactly like Kate's missing rollerball. In fact, Kel would have taken any bet that it *was* Kate's rollerball.

*You rat-bag!* he thought, inwardly seething. Whether Glenda had found the pen or stolen it, he didn't know; but it didn't matter either way – she had it, and she obviously didn't intend to give it back. Kel was half tempted to say something out loud, there and then, but just as his mouth started to open, he thought again. What if the pen *was* Glenda's? OK, it was an unusual colour and design, but Kate's wasn't the only one in existence. He couldn't start hurling accusations around without proof.

He was still dithering about it when suddenly Glenda looked up. She saw him, saw the expression on his face, and smiled. It was a smug, contemptuous smile, and it said clearly: *Yeah, it's Kate's pen. And you try proving it!*

*Right*, thought Kel. He couldn't do anything now, in front of the class, but Glenda wasn't going to get away with this.

He glanced at Chocky again, but the mynah bird appeared to have gone to sleep. Scowling, and gripping his own pen so hard that his knuckles turned pale, Kel turned back to his poem.

No one ever wanted to hang around after

one of Ms Shipton's lessons, so when it ended there was a general scramble for the door. As Glenda breezed past him, Kel said, in what he hoped sounded a casual way, "Hey, Glenda, hang on a minute."

She stopped. "Why?"

"I want a word."

"Oh, yeah?" That smile came back to her face. "What about?"

Ms Shipton had gone and the last of their classmates were piling out, so Kel could talk freely. "You know what about," he said. "Your pen. Or should I say Kate's?"

Glenda's smile didn't waver. "Sorry," she said, with just a hint of a sneer in her voice, "I've no idea what you're on about."

There wasn't any point playing games, Kel told himself. Better to come straight out with it.

"You've got Kate's pen," he said flatly. "I saw it." He held out one hand, palm up. "Give it to me, Glenda."

She pretended to be surprised, then pretended to understand. "Oh, *this* pen?" She produced it from her pocket and twirled it. "Sorry, Kel, you've made a mistake. This isn't Kate's. It's mine."

"You're a liar!" Kel said hotly. "No one else round here's got a pen like that!"

"They have now," said Glenda triumphantly.

Kel saw red. He made a grab for the pen, but Glenda snatched it away and raised it high. She was several centimetres taller than he was, and he couldn't reach for it without jumping up and down like a puppy. Glenda's smile became a broad grin.

"Sorry, kid. Your mistake. If you don't like it, why not go and tell the Head and see what he says?" He wouldn't, she knew. The Head didn't like telltales, and Kel couldn't prove a thing.

Twirling the pen one more time, Glenda sauntered towards the door. She looked back once, triumphantly – and as she did so the door opened and Kate came in.

"Come on, Kel, or we're going to be late for. . ." She stopped.

Glenda had reacted fast, shoving the pen back into her pocket, but Kate had glimpsed it and recognized it. Her mouth opened, but before she could utter another word, Glenda said, "See you," and was gone.

"Kel. . ." Kate stared after her. "She's got—"

"Your pen. Yeah. I know. But—"

A loud squawk interrupted him, and they both swung round to Chocky's cage.

Chocky was bouncing on his perch. The squawk turned into a piercing whistle – and then, in the weird, goo-goo little voice that gave Kel the creeps, he said: "Susie doesn't like that . . . *Atishoo!* Susie's going to get you! Susie's going to get you!"

Kate goggled. "Did you hear that?" she said.

Kel had heard, and wished he hadn't.

"It's almost as if he *understands*," Kate went on. She approached the cage. "Hey, Chocky, are you going to get Glenda, then? Going to get me my pen back?"

"Kate, don't!" Kel said sharply.

She threw him a withering look. "Don't be a prat! He's only a bird; he can't really understand. Can you, Chocky, eh?" She wiggled a finger for him and Chocky crooned at her.

"So who's Susie?" Kel demanded. His heart was bumping and he didn't want it to. He was starting to feel very wound up.

"Like I said yesterday, it's probably all down to Steve," said Kate. She paused, looking at him again. "Kel, what's the matter with you? You look scared!"

"Yeah." Kel's voice wasn't steady. "I think I am. Because I think something's going to happen to Glenda, just like it did to Ms Shipton."

"Oh, come on! That was an accident! How could it have anything to do with Chocky?"

Kel didn't know the answer to that question. But there *was* a connection. He was absolutely certain of it.

"Anyway," Kate added malevolently, "if something bad *does* happen to Glenda, I'm not going to cry about it. Nicking my pen! Chocky can't get her for it, but I can, and I tell you, Kel, I'm going to!"

"Glen-DA!" said Chocky. "Glen-DA!" It sounded like a peculiar and rather ugly little song.

"Come on." Kate took hold of Kel's arm, steering him towards the door. "You can help me plan my strategy in break."

She propelled him out. Chocky chuckled. It was a very human sound. Then, softly and thoughtfully, as if he was very pleased with himself, he said: "*Susie's* here. . ."

# 4

Kel was in a terrible state for the rest of the morning; jumpy as a firecracker and unable to concentrate on anything except the constant fear that something awful was going to happen.

The fact that nothing did happen only made matters worse. It was a bit like going to the dentist: he just wanted to get it over with, and it was the waiting that was shredding his nerves. But through the morning's lessons and the break in between, disaster didn't strike Glenda Parsons.

Glenda knew Kel was watching her (though

of course she didn't know the real reason why), and she made the most of it, taunting and baiting him whenever the chance arose. By lunchtime Kel felt like an overused dish-rag; wrung out and strung out and just about ready to jump off a cliff, if there'd been a cliff handy. He'd been chewed out by three different teachers for not listening, and when he'd tried to explain his fears to Steve and Kate, they both thought he was completely mad.

And Chocky hadn't said another word.

Kel trailed into the canteen wishing that he could blot this day out and start all over again. He wasn't hungry, but, nudged by Steve, he put a slice of pizza and a banana milk shake on his tray and drooped to a table as far away from the general chatter as he could get. Steve flopped down beside him and started devouring his own plateful. Kate was still in the queue, and Glenda was a few places ahead of her. Kel watched as Glenda took some fish fingers and a helping of chips, and Steve said, "Get a life, Kel! Stop *staring* at her. She isn't going to drop dead – worse luck."

Kel sighed, and tried to pull himself together. Steve was right; this was getting ridiculous. Just because Chocky had said what he had and then Ms Shipton had walked into the door, it didn't mean that the two things were linked. Like Kate had said, it was an accident. And Chocky was just a bird.

He started to eat his pizza. It tasted like rubber and cardboard with tomato sauce, but he forced himself to keep going, not wanting to face the afternoon on an empty stomach. Steve was talking about some TV programme he'd seen last night; Kel tried to listen but wasn't really taking any of it in. . .

There was a sudden commotion on the far side of the canteen.

It started with a godawful noise – a kind of rasping, retching sound. Then someone screamed, and within seconds chairs were scraping back and feet were pounding as people converged on one table in the corner.

"What's going on?"

"Who is it?"

"Oh God! She's—"

"Someone get the Head!"

"Someone get a doctor!"

The shouting voices all clashed confusedly together. And among them, driving into Kel's

34

ears and mind, was the hideous noise of some-one violently gagging.

He knew who it was without having to look, and he was on his feet and running towards the table, with Steve in pursuit. As he shoved his way through the gathering crowd, two faces registered on his brain. One was Kate's, and for an awful moment he thought *she'd* done it, until her blank, horrified expression made him realize that she was as shocked as anyone else.

The other face, swollen and purple and dis-torted with pain and terror, was Glenda's. She had a hand clamped to her throat, and she was choking.

The agitated voices swelled again. "Where's the Head? Get the Head!" "Loosen her clothes!" "Pull her hand away, thump her on the back!" "What's that thing they do where they squeeze and it comes out?" They were panicking, and Glenda was trying to scream but her throat was blocked and she could only make those terrible noises.

The doors crashed and the school secretary came running in. She took one look and barged through the throng like a battleship, shoving everyone else aside. Rigid with shock,

Kel could only watch as she grabbed Glenda from behind, locked her hands around her ribcage and, expertly, squeezed inwards and upwards. An appalling gargle echoed through the canteen. Something fell from Glenda's pocket, glinting momentarily and hitting the floor with a tiny, metallic sound.

And with a gasping, gurgling rush, the fishbone that had stuck in Glenda's throat came out, and she collapsed to the floor.

The next few minutes were a chaos of babbling voices and milling people, then the searing whine of an ambulance siren cut through the clamour and Glenda was whisked off to hospital. There was no real need, as the secretary had said; but it was better to be on the safe side, and if nothing else Glenda was suffering from shock.

She wasn't the only one, Kel thought as the uproar in the canteen at last began to die down. He, Steve and Kate were all standing together. They weren't talking: none of them wanted to be first to say what was in their mind. But after the medics carried Glenda away, Kate had bent and picked up the object that had fallen from her pocket as the secretary grabbed hold of her.

The pen. Kate held it in her hand now, her fingers fidgeting nervously up and down its length. At last, seeing that the boys weren't going to speak, she forced herself to break the silence.

She said: "What do you think Chocky's doing now. . .?"

Neither Kel nor Steve answered. Steve shuffled his feet, while Kel stared very hard at a smudged footprint on the floor.

"I mean," Kate went on, "someone ought to check. Oughtn't they?"

Steve shrugged. Kel went on staring at the smudge.

"Oh, come on, the pair of you!" Kate exploded suddenly. "We can't just ignore it!" She drew a deep breath. "All right, Kel, if it makes you feel any better, I believe you now. I've got to, haven't I? Once is coincidence, but twice isn't."

Kel looked up at last. "That's what I tried to tell you yesterday, only—"

"All right, I know, and I'm *sorry*. Look, I'm going to see Chocky. See what he's doing, see if he says anything. Are you two coming, or not?"

It had to be faced, Kel thought. "Yeah," he said. "I'll come."

"Kel. . ." Steve began. He was still trying to pretend that there wasn't anything weird about this, Kel realized. But after today's incident, that was starting to look crazier than believing it.

"You do what you want, Steve," he said. "But I'm going with Kate."

He didn't wait to see how Steve reacted, but followed Kate towards the door. After a second or two's hesitation, Steve followed.

There was no one in the classroom. Chocky's cage stood in its familiar place, and at first it looked as if he was asleep. But as they tiptoed towards the cage, the mynah bird raised his head. He looked at them perkily, almost cockily, and said, "Chocky biscuit? Be quiet at the back!"

Despite himself Kel smiled at the mimicry of Mrs Dwyer's favourite phrase. "Hi, Chocky," he said. *OK, here goes. . .* "Where's Susie?"

Chocky tilted his head first to one side and then to the other, as if weighing up the question. Then he whistled.

"Come on, Chocky. Where's Susie?"

"SusieSusie. SusieSusie." It wasn't the childish little voice, though, but Chocky's normal
tones. Kate, standing at Kel's shoulder, said
under her breath, "Never mind *where's* Susie –
I want to know *who* she is."

Chocky fixed a bright gaze on her, and
uttered an unpleasant giggle. The sound was so
unexpected that Kate and Kel both jumped
back, colliding with Steve who was keeping a
cautious distance.

"Ugh!" said Kate. "Did you *hear* that? It was
horrible!"

Chocky laughed again. Then, in the creepy
way that they both remembered all too well, he
intoned: "Susie says, *atishoo!*"

Atishoo. Chocky – or "Susie" – was always
saying it, and Kel was certain that it must be a
clue. But where did it lead? Who *was* Susie –
and how was she controlling the mynah
bird?

Approaching the cage again, he crouched
down so that his eyes were on a level with
Chocky's.

"Hey, Chocky," he said, quite gently. "You
know me, don't you? It's Kel. We're mates,
aren't we?"

Chocky chirped.

"Yeah, we're mates," Kel repeated. "So come on, tell me. Who's Susie, huh? Who is she?"

Chocky stared blankly at him, and Steve said uneasily, "Kel, don't be so stupid. He can't understand."

Kel waved a hand, shushing him. "Come on, Chocky, come on. Who's Susie? Tell me. Tell your mate Kel."

The bird only continued to look at him, and after a few more tries Kel had to admit defeat. Steve was right. Words didn't *mean* anything to Chocky; he only repeated what he heard people say.

So where had Susie's words come from?

Kel sighed and stood up. "OK, I give up," he said reluctantly. "This isn't going to work. We'll have to find another way to track Susie down."

Turning away from the cage, he started to walk towards the door. The others followed.

And Chocky said, quite clearly, "Susie won't hurt *you*."

They all stopped dead. Turned. Stared. Birds can't grin, but if Chocky had been human there would have been a smirk on his face.

"Susie won't hurt *you*," he repeated, then paused as if he was thinking – or listening to something no one else could hear. "Susie *likes* you."

"She likes us . . . ?" Kate echoed in a faint, shocked voice.

"She's got a funny way of showing it," Steve muttered.

Chocky glanced at him. "Atishoo!" he said. It sounded almost sarcastic.

Kel was just about to say, "Look, I think we ought to go somewhere else and talk about this," when the door opened and Joe Byrne, one of their classmates, came in.

"Oh, hi," he said. "What are you lot doing in here?"

Kel opened his mouth, but Chocky beat him to it.

"Go away!" he announced.

Joe laughed. "Hiya, Chocky! Sorry, mate, I haven't got a biscuit for you today."

"Go *away*," Chocky repeated. "Susie says. Go away."

"Oh, he's doing that again, is he?" said Joe. "Hey, what about Glenda, then? Everyone says it serves her right, but even so – OW!"

As he spoke, he'd been wagging a finger at the cage bars, making friendly overtures to Chocky but not looking at what he was doing. And Chocky had pecked him, hard.

Swearing, Joe nursed his finger, which was bleeding. "What's got into him?" he demanded. "He doesn't usually do things like that!"

"Joe," Kate said hollowly, "I think you'd better go. . ."

As if he understood, Chocky bounced on his perch and agreed: "Go away, go away, Susie says go away! Or else!"

Joe looked from Kate to Chocky and back to Kate again. "Too right, I'm going! For starters, I want a plaster for this!" He pointed his crimson-tipped finger at Chocky. "You try that again, bird, and you'll regret it!"

"*Sqwuaaark!*" Chocky retorted. "Atishoo, atishoo, Susie says *boo!*"

Joe had already turned and was heading for the door. No one could say quite how it happened, but at the same moment as the "Boo" he pulled the door open and, somehow, managed to lose his grip on the handle. The door came smacking back at him, too fast for anyone to shout a warning. And with an audible thud, the hard wooden edge hit him full in the face.

# 5

It wasn't much of an incident, as Kel, Steve and Kate all agreed later. Joe hadn't been badly hurt – a pecked finger and a couple of bruises, that was all. But no one had any doubts now. First Ms Shipton, then Glenda, now Joe. Two accidents *could* have been coincidence. Three wasn't. No way.

"Joe didn't even *do* anything," Steve said uneasily as they walked down the school drive at the end of the day. "I mean, telling Chocky he hadn't got a biscuit – hardly the crime of the century, is it?"

"I don't think the biscuit had anything to do

44

with it," said Kel. "Chocky – or Susie – told Joe to go away, and he didn't. That's what did it."

"You mean *that* was enough to make Susie mad?" asked Kate incredulously.

Kel nodded. "Looks that way."

Steve let out a soft, low whistle. "If you're right . . . Kel, this is getting serious!"

"Tell me about it!" Kel agreed with feeling. "I don't know how, but we've got to try and find out more about Susie – who she is, and how she's doing this."

Kate shivered. "She's got some kind of power, that's for sure. Controlling Chocky *and* making these things happen . . . it's scary."

"Do you think it *is* someone in the school?" Steve said.

Kel didn't answer immediately. He had the bones of an idea, but he wasn't sure that he wanted to reveal it to the others yet. They wouldn't want to get involved; they'd probably try to talk him out of it, and they might well succeed, because the prospect of trying it was pretty unnerving.

Kate and Steve's bus was trundling towards them (their homes were in the opposite direction to Kel's), and Kel made a snap decision. He wouldn't say anything to anyone, not yet. Today was Friday; over the weekend he'd do some careful thinking. And on Monday maybe he could try the experiment he had in mind. . .

Steve said, "Kel? Do you?"

Kel shook his thoughts off. "Think it's someone in the school? Yeah. Or at least – look, here's your bus. We'll talk on Monday, OK?"

"What about Chocky in the meantime?" Kate demanded.

"He'll be all right. There'll only be the caretaker going in to feed him, Susie won't do anything."

Kate might have argued, but the bus had stopped and the doors were opening. She and Steve climbed aboard, and Kel waved as the bus pulled away again. He didn't want to talk any more. He just wanted to get home, and start making plans.

Before assembly on Monday, Kel, Steve and Kate went to check on Chocky. They opened the classroom door – and stopped, staring at the empty space where his cage had been.

"Oh hell!" said Steve. "Where's he gone?"

"Someone must have moved him!" Kel

peered under the table, then started looking in cupboards, as if he expected to find Chocky lurking in some dark corner.

"Kel, don't be stupid," Kate said. "He isn't here." Hands on hips, she looked around her. "He's probably been taken back to the activity room. The workmen must have finished in there by now."

"We'd better go and check," Steve added.

They turned to leave – and came face to face with their class teacher. She was standing in the open doorway, glaring at them with a very suspicious expression on her face.

"Oh! Er . . . hello, Mrs Dwyer," said Kel desperately. "Is your cold better?"

"Yes, thank you, Kelvin," Mrs Dwyer replied frostily. "And what about you three? Looking for something, by any chance?"

"Well – um – we just wondered—"

"Where the bird is. Yes, I thought you might. Well, you may or may not be amused to know that I've had it taken back to the activity room, and that's where it'll stay from now on."

"Oh. . ." said Kate. "Er . . . can I ask why?"

Mrs Dwyer gave her a "don't-think-you-can-fool-me" look. "Because some person – or perhaps I should say some *people* – have been teaching it to say a lot of very coarse and childish things, which are not in the least bit amusing." She paused. "I don't know who's responsible, and I've got better things to do than waste my time finding out. But the joke stops here. Now," indicating the door with a nod of her head, "it's almost time for assembly, so you'd better get moving."

She stalked out, leaving them staring after her.

"What do you think Chocky said in front of her?" Kate asked after a few moments.

"God knows," said Kel. "But it looks like Susie didn't threaten anything, because she's still in one piece."

"So far," Steve put in gloomily.

"Oh, shut up! She said 'coarse and childish', so it was probably just that stupid rhyme about Mary Brown again. Come on. At least we know where Chocky is. And the activity room isn't being properly used yet, so he won't have much chance to do anything awful."

"You mean Susie won't," Kate corrected him ominously.

"Give it a rest, will you?" Kel glared at them

both. "You two are starting to sound like the Voices of Doom!" He felt edgy suddenly, because a small, unpleasant shiver had run down his spine. It always did, now, whenever Susie's name was mentioned, and he didn't like it. It was almost as if someone or something was answering to the name. Answering, and secretly giggling. . .

"Come on," he said again, annoyed with himself and with them. "We'll find Chocky at break. Till then, we'd better just keep our fingers crossed!"

At assembly, the Head droned on for some time about the forthcoming opening day for the school's new wing. Kel didn't bother to listen. The Head was one of those people who could make news of an alien landing sound boring, and Kel wasn't exactly ecstatic about the opening day in the first place. But when lessons started, he was in for an unpleasant surprise.

Mrs Dwyer was in her best sarcastic form – as Kate said later, she'd probably been saving up all the vitriol during her sick leave – and it wasn't long before she turned her attention to Kel.

"Kelvin." She smiled at him, like the croco-
dile in Peter Pan. "I'm sure you listened carefully to what Mr Wright said this morning?"

"Er – yes," Kel lied.

"Good. Then you'll know what I want you to
do about the mynah bird, won't you?"

Kel's blank expression was a total giveaway,
and Mrs Dwyer's face became triumphant. "I
see," she said. "Well, as you obviously had
more important things to think about, I'd better
jog your memory, hadn't I?"

Someone sniggered at the back, but a
gorgon look from the teacher silenced it.

"The school pets," she continued, "are to be
removed from the activity room, to make more
space for the parents and guests at the opening on Saturday. Some can be kept elsewhere
in the school for a while, but others will have to
be taken home by volunteers. And that bird is
at the top of the list."

Kel had an awful feeling he knew what was
coming next, and he was right.

"As you seem to spend more time talking to
the bird than listening in class, I'm giving you
the job of making the arrangements for it."
Her brows knitted together menacingly. "I

don't care where it goes, just so long as it is *out* of this school by the end of the week. Is that clear, Kelvin?"

Kel's jaw dropped. "But Mrs Dwyer, I *can't!*"

"Why not?"

"Because—" Then Kel stopped as he realized that he couldn't possibly tell her the real reason, and couldn't think up a plausible excuse in the next three seconds. Face paling, he turned his gaze down to the floor and mumbled, "Nothing. . ."

"Good." He could feel Mrs Dwyer's stare boring into him like a power-drill bit. "Then I'll expect to see the bird gone by Friday afternoon."

Kel nodded miserably. And anything else he might have felt was eclipsed by one single, horrible thought: *Susie's just going to love this. . .*

"What else could I do?" Kel snapped as he and Steve and Kate hurried along the corridor towards the activity room at break time. "She didn't give me any choice!"

"You could have said no!" Kate insisted. "I would have done."

"Oh, sure. And told her why, too, I suppose? 'Sorry, Mrs Dwyer, but it might make Susie angry and then she'll hurt someone.' Get real, Kate!"

"What I want to know is," Steve muttered, "who *is* going to take Chocky home? 'Cos I tell you, it won't be me!"

"Thanks," said Kel. "Some friend *you* are!"

"Well, it won't," Steve insisted. "Not for anything. Say the wrong thing and I end up in hospital – great!"

"I agree," said Kate. "I'm not having him either."

Sudenly Kel had had enough. He stopped walking and glowered at them both. "This is getting stupid!" he snapped. "We don't even know for sure that something weird *is* happening."

"Oh, come on—" Kate began.

"No, *listen*. It could still be coincidence, couldn't it? We haven't actually *proved* anything at all. So before we get totally paranoid, I reckon we should try a couple of experiments."

"Oh?" Kate eyed him warily. "What sort of experiments?"

Kel had been thinking hard over the weekend and in class this morning, and he had a plan of sorts worked out. It was a bit risky, but in the absence of anything better it would have to do. Anyway, he reflected, it wasn't as if he was going to ask Kate and Steve to be the guinea pigs. He'd do it himself.

Though they might have to pick up the pieces afterwards. . .

"Let's find Chocky," he said. "Then I'll show you."

The activity room was deserted, but as soon as they went in Chocky saw them and bounced on his perch.

"Chocky biscuit!" he squawked. "Three-two-one, Houston we have a problem!"

Despite jangling nerves, Kel smiled. "Hey, Chocky!" he greeted the mynah bird. "How you doing, huh?"

Chocky ruffled his wings and made crooning noises. It certainly didn't sound as if Susie was around, and Kel felt relieved. Being honest with himself, he admitted that he hadn't relished the idea of his experiment. Truthfully, *really* truthfully, the prospect scared the living daylights out of him, and he'd be only too glad to put it off.

Steve and Kate, unaware of his thoughts, were watching him uncertainly, waiting for him to do something but not knowing what it would be. Kel went over to Chocky's cage and examined the bird's food and water dishes.

"He's eaten everything," he said. "Steve, where's the bird seed? I'll refill his bowl."

At that moment, unexpectedly, Kate sneezed.

Chocky put his head on one side. His beady gaze fixed on Kate's face and he said, "A-TISH-oo!" There was a moment's pause. Then, in a completely changed voice, he added: "Susie says, bless you."

Steve said softly, "Oh-oh. . ." and a cold, liquid feeling clutched at Kel's stomach as he recognized the little-girly voice. Susie's voice.

He drew a deep breath. It was now or never; if he chickened out, he'd never find enough courage to try again another time.

*So*, he thought, feeling like someone with a bad head for heights about to make a parachute jump, *here goes*. . .

"Susie," he said aloud, slowly and carefully, "You're boring, and you're a nuisance. We don't want you hanging around any more. Go away, Susie. Go away – right *now*!"

# 6

There was an appalling silence. It probably lasted less than a minute, but to Kel it felt like half a lifetime. He was aware of Steve and Kate staring at him in speechless disbelief, and aware, too, of Chocky, who had turned his attention from Kate and was swaying from side to side on his perch, as if he was weighing up two things in his mind and couldn't decide between them.

Then, with a violent movement that made them all jump, he flapped his wings against the cage bars and cried raucously,

"*Spit-belly-bum-drawers!*"

"*What*?" It was so ludicrous that the awful tension vanished in an instant. Kate clapped a hand over her mouth, snorting, Steve stared in astonishment at Chocky, and Kel started to giggle and then found he couldn't stop.

"Where—" he gasped at last through tears of hilarity, "where on earth – did he learn – *that*?"

"Spitbellybumdrawers!" Chocky repeated, sounding thoroughly pleased with himself.

Kate shrieked with laughter. "M-my great-gran used to say that when she was little!" she cackled. "She told me – they were the rudest words she knew!"

The mynah bird's outburst was so funny – and such a huge relief after their fear of what might have happened – that they didn't notice that the voice Chocky had used was still Susie's. And when he spoke again, the tone – Susie's tone – was very, very different.

"Mustn't be horrid to Susie. . ." The sheer menace got through to them now, and abruptly their laughter started to fade. "Susie says no. Susie says *no*. . ."

Kel's heart gave a thumping lurch. "Cut it out, Chocky," he whispered.

But Chocky took no notice. "Susie says no. . ." Then without warning the childish voice rose to a furious screech: "Susie says no, NO, *NO!!*"

What happened next was so unexpected, so *impossible*, that Kel had no chance to prepare for it. Out of nowhere, out of nothing, an enormous, invisible force slammed into him. With a yell of terror Kel flailed, but his legs were whisked from under him, his hands grabbed at empty air, and he was flung across the room, crashing against a table and sprawling as it collapsed on top of him showering him with its contents.

"*Kel!*" Kate and Steve swept debris aside and pulled him out from under the table top. "Are you all right?" Kate cried.

"Uhh. . ." Kel felt dizzy and a bit sick, but it was more shock than anything else; miraculously, he didn't seem to be injured. "I'm OK," he said through clenched teeth. Kate tried to help him to his feet, but he shook her off and got up unaided. "Bit wobbly, that's all. Phew. . ."

"What *happened*?" Steve asked.

"I dunno. Something just – hit me. Like a

whirlwind." He looked at their faces. "You must have felt it!"

They shook their heads. "All I saw was you flying through the air," Kate told him. She glanced at the table. "We'd better try and pick it all up before anyone comes in."

"No way," said Steve. "I'm not hanging around here!" He pointed at Chocky's cage. "You heard what he said! It was Susie – *she* did that to Kel!"

Chocky watched them. He was silent now, but he was hunched broodingly, almost threateningly on his perch, and Kel felt fear crawl like spiders in his mind.

"Steve's right," he said in a hollow voice. "It *was* Susie. And this time, she wasn't messing about."

That was more than enough for Steve. "I'm going!" he said. "You two can do what you want, but count me out!"

Kate shouted after him, but he was already through the door, and they could hear his feet pounding along the passage. Chocky crooned. It sounded more like his normal self, but without words it was impossible to be sure.

"We ought to clear up. . ." Kate said faintly.

"No." Kel backed away from the cage. "Leave it, Kate. No one saw us come in here; they won't know who did it." Even if they found out, he'd rather face ten furious Mrs Dwyers than spend another moment anywhere near Susie. "Come on." He took hold of her arm, tugging her towards the door.

"But what – I mean, how did she—"

"I don't know any more than you do! And right now I don't want to." He pulled again. Kate resisted. She stared at Chocky in his cage, and in a shaking voice she said, "Susie . . . Kel didn't mean it. Please, Susie, please stop doing these things. . ."

Chocky tilted his head and blinked. "Spitbellybumdrawers!" he announced.

It wasn't funny any more. It sounded more like someone having a sulky tantrum.

Or delivering a warning.

Kate shuddered, then after one more frightened glance in the direction of the cage she hurried out of the room on Kel's heels.

There was trouble when the mess in the activity room was discovered. But everyone in the school denied knowing anything about it, and the only three who weren't telling the truth managed to keep up a reasonable pretence of innocence. Mrs Dwyer suspected them, they knew, but she couldn't prove anything, so they were safe enough.

From her, at least. But Susie was another matter.

Kate was the only one of them who mustered enough courage to face Chocky again that day. She actually volunteered to help clear up the mess, and when Kel and Steve told her she was out of her mind, she said: "Don't be dumb; I don't *want* to do it! But one of us ought to be there, to make sure Susie doesn't get angry again." She fished a handful of sweets out of her pocket. "I'm taking these with me. Sort of peace offering."

"For *Susie*?" Steve was incredulous. "You think she can eat *sweets*?"

"No, of course I don't! But Chocky can, and she might get the message."

Steve thought the idea was totally crazy, but Kel didn't get involved in the argument. He had a sneaking feeling that Kate's tactic might just work. And when they all had a chance to talk again in the canteen, it seemed he was right. Chocky had apparently greeted the clear-up crew with a barrage of near-hysterical squawks, "Atishoos" and "Spitbellybum-drawers". Everyone else thought it was hilarious, but Kate quickly gave him the sweets, whispering to him as she did so, and almost immediately he calmed down.

"There wasn't another word about Susie," she told Kel and Steve. "He just whistled, and sang football chants – all the things he used to do before this started."

Steve let out a long breath. "Do you reckon we've heard the last of Susie, then?"

Kate looked at Kel. Kel knew what she was thinking, and he let her see that he felt the same.

"No way," they said.

Kel was in his room that evening when the phone rang and his mum called up the stairs: "Kel! It's for you."

He came downstairs and Mum said, "It's Kate, from school." A pause. "She sounds a bit excited. What have you been up to?"

Mum always assumed that he was "up to" something, but for once Kel didn't rise to the bait. "Thanks, Mum," was all he said, and picked up the receiver. "Kate? Hi – what's up?"

"Is anyone else listening?" Kate asked.

Kel glanced over his shoulder. Mum was hovering, but if this didn't sound interesting she'd soon go away. "It's fine," he said, making his voice sound casual. "How's the project going?"

"OK, I get it – you can talk but you've got to be a bit careful. Listen, then, and just say yes or no. Do you know what a poltergeist is?"

The creeping, spidery sensation that Kel had felt in his mind that morning came back with a vengeance. He knew the word, he'd heard it before; and though he couldn't remember exactly what it meant, he knew it had something to do with hauntings.

Casting another quick, furtive glance along the hall (Mum was still hanging around), he said, "Sort of . . . but clue me in a bit."

"Right. Basically – this is what I know from films and stuff – they're malevolent forces or something, and what they do is *move* things. Throw them around, you know; like ornaments or bits of furniture." Kate paused significantly. "Or even people."

"Ouch. . ." said Kel.

"Precisely. Just like what happened to you this morning."

"You think Susie might be—" *Careful, Kel*, "working like that?" he finished.

"Yeah, I do. So I went into the town library on my way home, to see if I could find out a bit more."

Another pause. "And did you?" Kel asked at last.

"Yeah," said Kate again. "Kel, I – I think I've worked out what Susie is."

"Go on."

The third pause was the longest of all, and Kel would have given anything to be able to see Kate's face and get an idea of her thoughts. Finally, she spoke again.

"I think," she said, "that Susie is a person. A human being. Or rather, she was. Because she's dead. She's come back to haunt us – and she's taken control of Chocky. He's possessed, Kel. He's possessed by Susie. And Susie's not just a ghost; she's a poltergeist as well!"

# 7

Facing Chocky the next day wasn't going to be the easiest thing Kel had ever done. And the phone conversation with Kate had made him feel even more nervous.

Poltergeists. Malicious spirits that caused havoc and disruption, that could move things, throw things, hurt people. . . It fitted the picture they were getting of Susie with a horrible kind of inevitability.

But where had Susie come from? And why had she suddenly appeared? Those were the two most baffling questions nagging in Kel's mind as he got off the bus outside the school gates and walked apprehensively up the drive. He and Kate had talked about that last night, but neither of them had come up with any ideas. Afterwards, Kel had thought of ringing Steve to sound him out. But he'd decided against it. Steve was already scared enough; it would be better to get him face to face, and with Kate as backup, before telling him about their theory.

Morning lessons were punctuated by banging and crashing from the new school hall. Apparently (the Head must have said this yesterday, but Kel hadn't been listening) an exhibition of the school's history was being set up in there – something to impress the Big Noises on the opening day. The workmen were making an enormous racket, but the hall doors were firmly shut, and anyway, Kel was too preoccupied to be interested in whatever was going on in there.

When break time came, Steve disappeared. Kel and Kate tried everywhere they could think of, but couldn't find him.

"He's avoiding us," Kate said sourly. "After yesterday, when he chickened out, he's too ashamed to face us."

"Or too scared," Kel pointed out.

"Both, probably." She scowled. "OK, who needs him anyway? We can't afford to waste time. Let's go and find Chocky."

Kel hesitated. "I don't think that's such a good idea."

"Huh?" Kate stared, incredulous. "What's the matter with you, Kel? You're not bottling out too, are you?"

"It's all right for you," Kel argued. "It wasn't you that Susie attacked!"

"She won't do it again."

"Says who?"

"Look, Kel, I gave Chocky those sweets yesterday and it did the trick. Susie's calmed down, and I know she won't hurt you again unless you do something to upset her. We've got to try and find out more about her. And if you haven't got the guts to come, I'll do it on my own!"

That stung, and although he knew it was exactly what Kate wanted, Kel rose to the bait. They headed for the activity room, where Chocky was waiting for them. Someone else had been in, because the mynah bird's food dish was full and there were the remains of a chocolate biscuit on the cage floor. But there hadn't been any trouble, and Chocky greeted them with a cheerful squawk that sounded like his normal self.

"Hello, Chocky." Kate went up to the cage and crouched down so that her face was on a level with the bird's. Chocky made a noise that sounded like someone blowing a raspberry and said, "Be quiet at the back!"

Ignoring that, Kate said gently, "Chocky, where's Susie? Hello, Susie. What does Susie say?"

There was a long silence. Kel had the uncomfortable feeling that something invisible was watching him.

Then Chocky announced: "A-TISH-oo!"

"She's here. . ." Kate glanced quickly at Kel, who fought down a queasy feeling.

"She might not be," he whispered. "Chocky doesn't only say that when she's around."

He was hoping desperately that he was right and Kate was wrong – but a second later his hopes were dashed, because Chocky added clearly, "Susie says, Atishoo! Susie says, Bless you!"

Kate looked at him again. "See, Susie?

Here's Kel. He's not horrible; he's nice really. You like him, don't you?"

Chocky sidled along his perch in Kel's direction, and the bright eyes fixed on his face. Then: "Say sorry!"

"What?"

Chocky whistled shrilly. "Say sorry! Susie says, Susie says! Atishoo!"

"She wants you to apologize for what you did yesterday," Kate hissed. "Do it, Kel, quickly! Before she gets annoyed!"

Kel gulped, and scrabbled for words. "Sorry, Susie!" he said hastily. "I didn't mean what I said."

"Tell her you like her and you want to be her friend!"

Kel swallowed again. Something seemed to be sticking in his throat and he had to make a huge effort. "I want to be your friend, Susie. I like you, honest – I like you lots!"

Chocky's feathers had started to ruffle, but abruptly they settled and smoothed down again. He chirped.

"Let's be friends, Susie," Kel cajoled, wondering if this was some godawful dream. *If it is, let me wake up soon, oh, please!*

"Atishoo!" said Chocky again. "Atishoo, atishoo, Susie says atishoo!"

What did that mean? Was he forgiven or not?

Then suddenly Chocky said: "Atishoo, atishoo, weallfalldown!"

"That's a new one," Kate whispered. "The kids' nursery rhyme . . . she's never done that before." She put a finger through the cage bars and stroked Chocky's back. "Susie? Do you know the song?" And she started to sing: "Ring a ring of roses, a pocket full of—"

She didn't get a chance to finish. "*NO!*" Chocky squawked. "NoNO, noNO, noNO – ATISHOO, ATISHOO!"

"Stop it, Kate! She doesn't like it!" Kel flapped his hands frantically to shut her up. "Sorry, Susie, sorry! She won't sing it again, promise!"

"NoNO." But the voice was calmer now. There was a pause. Then Chocky said, "Atishoo. Susie says, bless you. Bless you. Bless Susie. Bless school. Allfalldown."

Kate's face was a picture of bafflement. "Whatever's all that about?" she asked.

Kel shook his head. "Search me. I can't make any sense of it."

"Hey, Susie." Kate stroked Chocky again. "What do you mean, Susie, huh? Bless Susie? Bless school?"

But Chocky didn't answer. His head had sunk on to his chest and he shut his eyes, rocking slightly on the perch and looking like someone pretending to be asleep.

A bell rang somewhere in the depths of the school, and Kate frowned. "Oh, rats! That's break over!" She straightened up. "We'll have to come back later."

"I think she's gone anyway," Kel said. "Chocky looks . . . different, somehow. More normal."

"Yeah, I know what you mean. It's weird, but he *does* change when Susie's around. Come on. We'll leave things to settle down till lunchtime. Then I've got an idea."

"What sort of idea?" Kel asked.

"I want to think it over first. And I want to tackle Steve. What I've got in mind might need all three of us."

And she wouldn't tell him any more.

* * *

Steve proved hard to corner, but they did it eventually, and a mixture of nagging and threats persuaded him to listen to what they had to say.

Though at first he was reluctant to admit it, Steve agreed with the poltergeist theory. But after what had happened during break, Kel and Kate now had something else to add.

"Susie's not just any old poltergeist," Kate said, ignoring the astonished gargling noise Steve made at her choice of words. "We think she's got a reason for coming here."

"We reckon she used to be at this school," Kel added. He and Kate had hit on this on their way back from the activity room. "Bless Susie, bless school" – it seemed to make sense; as if the ghost or geist or whatever Susie was missed the school and wanted to come back.

"Trouble is," Kate went on, "we don't know when she was here, and without that we haven't got much chance of finding out who she was or what she's doing here now."

"Oh, come on!" Steve said explosively. "We know exactly what she's doing – making trouble and scaring the hell out of us!"

"Shut up and *listen*, will you?" said Kate.

"There's got to be more to it than that. There's got to be a *reason* why Susie's come back."

She and Kel told Steve about their attempt, during break, to communicate properly with Susie for the first time. "We didn't get very far, though," Kel finished. "She just started saying silly things, nursery rhymes and stuff. We couldn't get any proper answers."

"I think Chocky might be the problem," said Kate.

Kel looked at her keenly. "Chocky? Why?"

"He's only a bird, right? OK, so Susie's controlling him and making him come out with all these things—"

"We *think*," Steve interrupted. "No one's proved it yet."

Kate shot him a filthy look. "If you want to be picky—"

"I only said—"

"Shut up, the pair of you!" Kel was running out of patience. "If Susie isn't controlling Chocky, then everything we've thought so far's a load of rubbish. So let's say she is. Go on, Kate."

"Well." Kate looked and sounded very mysterious. "Like I said, Chocky's only a bird.

So there's probably a limit to what Susie can do through him."

Steve's eyes rolled. "Thank God for that!"

"All *right*! I was thinking of what she says, not what she does. What if she *wants* to talk to us properly, but she can't, because Chocky isn't the right sort of. . ." She waved her hands around. "What's the word?"

"Conductor?" Kel suggested. He was suddenly very interested in Kate's idea.

"Yeah, that's it. Like in chemistry, when we did that thing about different materials conducting heat. Some do, some don't. Susie needs a better conductor than Chocky. If we can get her one, we might find out what's *really* going on."

A small worm of excitement was squirming in Kel's stomach. "Hey," he said softly, "that could work."

Steve, though, was much less enthusiastic. "Sure it could, if Kate's right about Chocky. But what are we going to use? Because I've got a nasty feeling I know what you're thinking, Kate, and I'm telling you now: no way am I going to let myself in for that!"

"What do you mean?" Kel didn't understand.

"I mean, she's going to say that one of *us* should be the conductor or whatever you want to call it."

"I'm not saying anything of the sort!" said Kate. "D'you think I'm a complete idiot? No, I've had a different idea. But I'm not going to tell you what it is yet."

"Why not?"

"Because there isn't time to actually do it before lessons start again. And if I tell you about it before we do it, then you'll think of a million reasons why we shouldn't."

Neither Kel nor Steve liked the sound of that, and said so. But Kate was unrelenting. She wouldn't tell them any more, and she wasn't going to listen to any arguments. If they wanted to find out what she was planning, she said, then they'd have to come to the activity room with her after school. Until then, they could just keep guessing.

Kel told himself he wasn't going to go. It wasn't just that he resented being bamboozled by Kate; he also had an ominous feeling that whatever she was planning would lead to trouble. Not just ordinary trouble, either, but something far too big, and too dangerous, for them to handle. Kate was playing with fire and Kel didn't want to get burned along with her.

But his curiosity got the better of him, and so did Steve's. They both admitted that, whatever Kate's plan led to, they'd rather know the worst than have to imagine it.

"Anyway," Steve said gloomily, "Kate'll go ahead whatever we say, so I suppose we've got to be there to protect her."

Kel winced inwardly to think what Kate would have said to that piece of sexism, but he just nodded. "Yeah. And if she wants to do something really crazy, we can stop her."

Steve looked at him cynically. "Oh, sure," he said.

Kate was already in the activity room. When the boys went in they found her sitting at a table, cutting up some pieces of paper. Chocky watched her with apparent interest from his cage; he greeted Kel and Steve with a whistle then turned his attention to Kate again.

"Hi," Kate said, without looking up. "I'm nearly ready."

"Ready for what?" Kel asked.

"My plan." Kate made one last snip with the

scissors, then pushed the pieces of paper together in a neat stack. "There. All finished."

Steve frowned at the stack. "What are those?"

She picked them up, fanning them through her hands. On each piece of paper, a different letter of the alphabet was written.

Then Kel saw the cleared space on the table by Chocky's cage. In the middle of the space was an upturned drinking glass.

"Oh, no. . ." he said in a shocked voice. "Kate, we're not going to. . ."

The words trailed off, and Kate turned round on her stool to give him a challenging glare. "Yes," she said. "That's *exactly* what we're going to do." She brandished the pieces of paper at him. "We're going to see if we can talk to Susie ourselves – and *properly*!"

# 8

"You're out of your mind!" Kel had never felt so furious in his life, and the fact that the fury was caused mostly by fear made him more angry still. "If you think I'm getting involved in that sort of stuff, you can think again, Kate Ransome!"

"It's not just stupid, it's dangerous!" Steve agreed vehemently.

"All right, all *right!*" Kate was getting furious herself. "That isn't what I meant! I'm not talking about calling up spirits—"

"Oh, no? What's Susie, then, if she's not a spirit?"

"I mean, not calling anything up! Susie's already here – we didn't call her, but she is! Don't you understand? All I'm trying to do is give her another way to talk to us, and this was the only thing I could think of!"

They had quite a row about it, and it was lucky that the noise of their shouting didn't bring anyone to investigate. But it didn't, and eventually they all calmed down and agreed on a compromise.

Kate had to acknowledge that the stuff with the upturned glass wasn't a good idea. But at the same time, Kel and Steve admitted that the paper letters might help Susie to express herself more clearly. The best thing, they decided, was simply to spread the letters out on the table, and let Susie find her own way of spelling things out. They wouldn't touch the glass. They'd just sit back and watch.

Chocky was silent. In fact he hadn't made a sound all through the row and the calmer discussion afterwards. That was strange; noise usually got him excited, and they'd have expected him to squawk and whistle and shout along with them. The fact that he hadn't was more than a little unnerving.

As Kate started to lay the letters out, Kel said, "I wish there was a way of locking this door. If anyone came in now—"

"I wouldn't lock it if you paid me," countered Steve edgily. "We might want to get out in a hell of a hurry."

Kate gave him a scornful look. "If you're chicken—" she began.

"I'm not: I'm just sane. Which is more than I can say for you."

Chocky said: "Spitbellybumdrawers."

They all froze at the unpleasantly familiar sound of Susie's voice, and looked round to see the mynah bird hunched menacingly, staring at them.

"You shouldn't have said that, Steve," Kel muttered. "Susie doesn't like it."

Chocky made a hissing sound, and Kate added, "Say you're sorry, *quickly*!"

White-faced, Steve gabbled, "Sorry, Susie, sorry – I didn't mean it!"

"How long do you think she's been here?" Kel whispered to Kate.

"I don't know. Maybe since we came in."

In which case she already knew what they were going to do. Kel shivered. How would she react when they started trying to ask her questions? If she didn't like it. . .

Kate's voice broke into his unpleasant speculations as she laid down the last paper letter. "All set," she said tensely. The letters were arranged in three rows on the table, and Steve said, "How're we going to know which one Susie wants?"

Kate chewed her lip. "She might have her own way of showing us. Or we could try putting a pointer of some kind there, and she can move it." She looked around and found a bright yellow pencil. "This'll do."

They all stared at the layout, and Kel said, "How do we start?"

"We should talk to her," said Kate. She leaned towards Chocky's cage. "Hello, Susie. My name's Kate, and the boys are called Kel and Steve."

"I think she's worked that one out for herself," Steve said sarcastically.

"*Shh*. Susie, we'd like to know more about you. Can you point to the letters for us?"

Nothing happened. Chocky sat on his perch, gazing back at them, but he didn't make a sound. After a minute or so of silence, Kate tried again.

"Susie, where have you come from? Where do you live?"

"Zilch," Steve murmured after another long wait. "This isn't going to work."

"Hang on a minute," said Kel. "Maybe she doesn't realize what we want her to do? Show her, Kate. Point to some letters yourself, and see if that helps."

Kate nodded. She picked up the pencil and pointed one by one to the letters, saying her greeting aloud as she spelled it out.

"Hello, Susie."

Chocky gurgled, like water going down a plughole. He half-spread his wings.

And out of the corner of his eye, Kel saw the upturned glass, which they'd pushed to one side, move.

"Kate. . ." He touched her arm.

"Hang on; I'm trying to concentrate." She had started to spell out "Hello Susie" again, but before she got past the "E" of "Hello" Kel saw the glass move a second time.

"*Kate!* Something's happening!"

"Kel, will you stop—" Then the words broke off as Kate saw for herself. Slowly but surely, the glass was sliding across the table. It moved in odd little jerks, as though someone couldn't quite get hold of it. Then it stopped. They all held their breath, watching, but seconds passed and the glass didn't move again.

"Maybe we imagined it?" Steve whispered hopefully.

"No way," said Kel. "That was Susie. It *had* to be."

Kate turned eagerly back to the letters. "Come on, Susie," she coaxed. "Try and talk to us."

"SusieSusie. SusieSusie." Chocky started to rock from side to side on his perch. "Mary Brown went to town. *Atishoo!*"

"She's still trying to talk through Chocky," said Kate. "Come on, Susie; Chocky's only a bird. Try this instead." She started to tap the letters with the pencil. "H-E-L-L-O-S-U—"

"*NYAAAAAA!!*" Chocky's shriek was so sudden and violent that they all jumped back with yells of shock. Kate felt something grab the other end of the pencil; she screamed in terror as it pulled, hard, then the pencil was snatched out of her grasp. It twisted in the air, spinning – then with a loud *crack* it snapped in half, and the two pieces were hurled away in opposite directions.

"*Look out!*" Steve yelled.

As the broken pencil whirled away, the glass had skidded across the table and shot off the edge. It flew upwards, turning over and over – then with enormous force and energy it came hurtling straight at Kate's head. Kate ducked, only just in time, and the glass zoomed past the end of her nose.

"SPITBELLYBUMDRAWERS!" Chocky screeched. "Susie says, NO! Susie says, NO!"

The glass jerked to a halt in mid-air and hung there, half a metre above their heads. Some mad instinct made Kel try to reach for it, but Kate shouted, "*Don't!*" and Steve snatched at his arm, dragging him back.

"*Atishoo!*" squawked Chocky. "*Atishoo, atishoo, Susie says atishoo! Allfalldown! Allfalldown!*"

He started to flap his wings, beating them against the bars of the cage and shrieking raucously, though there were no words now. "Susie, stop it!" Kel cried. "Leave him alone, he'll hurt himself!"

He made to run towards Chocky's cage – and the glass, which was still suspended in empty air, twisted round and rocketed towards him. It hit him a glancing blow on the skull, then ricocheted across the room and smashed straight into the wall. It exploded like a small bomb, sending glittering shards flying everywhere, and as the fragments shattered a blast of ice-cold air tore across the room. Kate's letters were snatched up like dead leaves in a gale, and following them came other things: paper, books, pens and pencils – anything small that wasn't tied down. Year Three's hamster cage tipped over with a thud, waves sloshed on the surface of the fish tank, and suddenly Chocky's cage started to tilt and shake wildly on the table, as though huge, invisible hands had picked it up and were shaking it violently.

"Chocky!" Dodging an airborne book that was rebounding from the walls like a boomerang, Kel dived for the cage. Chocky was hysterical now, screeching and whistling and cawing, his wings a blur of movement as he flapped in panic. Kel grabbed the cage – but whatever had hold of it first was ten times stronger than he was. His arms were pulled almost out of their sockets as he tried to stop the shaking and pounding. Kate, who had run to pick up the hamster cage, saw and came to help, but it was useless.

"Steve!" Kel yelled above the din and mayhem. "Do something! Help us!"

"He's hiding under the table!" Kate shouted. "Leave him, he's useless!"

There was only one way to rescue Chocky, Kel realized. Panting and grunting as he battled against the malevolent force, he gasped, "Got to – get – Chocky – out! Try to – open the door, and I'll – grab him!"

Through her streaming hair he saw Kate nod. She fumbled with the door catch. It was stiff, and for a few moments he thought that she wouldn't be able to release it – but suddenly it came free, and the door jerked open. Kel thrust his arms into the cage. His groping hands reached for Chocky. But in his terror Chocky saw him only as another threat, and his beak stabbed like a knitting needle into the soft flesh between Kel's thumb and forefinger. Kel howled with pain; instinctively he snatched his hands back, out of the bird's reach – and in a flurry of black feathers Chocky fluttered out of the cage.

"Oh, no!" Kate screamed. "Catch him, *catch him*!"

She made a despairing grab, but she was far too slow. Chocky flew straight for the highest shelf in the room and crash-landed on it with an outraged "*KAA-AAAK!*" Kate tried to climb after him, but a sweep of his wings sent half the shelf's contents raining down on her and she backed off hastily, colliding with Kel who was still dazedly nursing his stabbed hand.

Then without any warning, the mayhem was over. One instant there was wild chaos, the next – it simply stopped. Stunned and blinking, Kel and Kate watched as a few last papers floated gently to rest on the floor. They made a tiny, rustling noise as they landed, and then there was utter silence.

They looked at each other disbelievingly. Kate opened her mouth but couldn't think of a thing to say. Kel was too gobsmacked to think at all.

Then from the shelf, very softly, Chocky spoke.

"Susie doesn't like that. Susie says *naughty*."

Kel felt as if someone had dunked him into a bath full of ice cubes. "Chocky. . ." he said. "Come on, Chocky; come on, boy. Come down. Come to Kel."

"A. . .*TISH*. . .oo." Chocky drew the word out, as if he was savouring it. His tone – or Susie's – was very unpleasant indeed.

"We've got to get him back," Kate said in an undertone.

"I know. But how? He's got wings. And a sharp beak." Kel rubbed his hand again.

Kate was thinking. "We need a net or something. And a stepladder." She swung round and peered under the tables. "Steve! Come out of there and stop being so spineless! We need your help!"

Steve's head emerged cautiously from under the table. "I'm not going near that bird!"

"All right, you don't have to! Go and find a net and a stepladder!"

"Huh? Where am I supposed to—"

"I don't *care*; just *find* them! Or something else that'll do!"

Steve hesitated. "Is he going to attack me?"

"No – but I am, if you don't shift!" Kate told him ferociously. "And whatever you do, don't let Chocky out of this room!"

"OK. . ." With a wary eye on the high shelf Steve crawled out of hiding and stood up. "I'll try the cupboard in the other corridor. . ." he

mumbled, heading for the door and opening it.
"And if that's no good, I'll—"

"*Steve!*"

Kel yelled the warning, but he was too late.
As Steve dithered in the doorway, Chocky saw
his chance and took it. What looked like a
small black whirlwind launched itself from the
shelf and arrowed towards the door. Kel and
Kate both leaped to slam it, but they were too
far away; and Steve, who would have been
close enough, was too confused to react at all.
He gawped as Chocky flew over his head. . .

And with a cry that sounded terrifyingly like
a nasty little kid's laugh, the mynah bird hurtled
triumphantly to freedom.

# 9

"There he goes!" Kel called, as a flapping dark shape vanished down the corridor. Not waiting for the others he ran in pursuit, skidded round a corner—

And cannoned straight into a man in overalls, carrying a large wooden board.

"What the—" The man collected himself, and shot out a hand to steady Kel as he nearly went sprawling. He grinned. "Where's the fire?"

Chocky had vanished and, winded, Kel gasped, "Bird – he got away, and –"

"The crow, or whatever it is? Yeah, I just saw it."

"He's a mynah bird," said Kate, hurrying up with Steve at her heels. "Which way did he go?"

The man jerked a thumb over his shoulder. "It was heading that way." The grin widened. "Going a bit faster than you lot, too."

"Oh, *no*! If he gets out of the building—"

"I shouldn't worry," said the workman. "Outside doors are all shut. It's probably gone into the new hall – but you can't go in there. We're setting up the exhibition stuff, and you kids are supposed to stay out."

"Oh, please!" Kate begged. "We've *got* to catch him!"

"Anyway," Kel said with a flash of inspiration, "he could cause trouble in there, couldn't he? Knock things over, make a mess."

"Well . . . oh, all right, go on, then. But you'd better hurry up and catch the thing, that's all. We're too busy to muck around with escaped pets!"

With shouts of "Thanks!" they ran on towards the hall and rushed in together.

The hall was a muddle of ladders, wires, trestle tables and cardboard boxes, with four more men working there. Two of them were stringing lighting cable around the wall. But the other two were on the far side of the hall, staring up at something by the platform.

Then, echoing eerily in the big space, an all too familiar voice said: "A-TISH-oo!"

"Chocky!" Running to where the men were standing, Kel looked up and saw the mynah bird. Chocky was perched on a high ledge, almost at roof level, peering down at the humans below.

"It's a rook," said one of the men.

"Nah!" said the other. "Too big. Looks more like a raven to me."

"He's a mynah bird, and his name's Chocky, and he's escaped," Kate told them. "We've got to get him back – can you help us?"

The man Kel had collided with had followed them into the hall by this time and, putting his board down, came over.

"You kids got any bird seed or anything?" he asked. "If it's tame, it might come down for food."

"He likes chocolate biscuits best," Kel said. "But I don't think he's very interested in eating at the moment."

From his high perch Chocky announced loudly, "Spitbellybumdrawers!" The workmen laughed, but Kel winced inwardly. Susie only said that when she was angry.

"Come on, Chocky!" he called. "Come to Kel! Chocky biscuit?"

"Spit!" said Chocky again. "Susie says spit, spit, spit. Atishoo!"

There was more laughter, but the man with the board said, "We haven't got time for this lark. Get a ladder, Alec, and go up there after it."

Chocky watched while the ladder was leaned against the wall. He didn't move as the man called Alec started to climb towards him.

"Here, birdie." Alec held a hand out. "Come on, then."

Chocky tilted his head to one side. "Susie says, *no!*"

Kel thought, *Oh-oh*. And Kate called anxiously, "Be careful!"

"All right, love, he knows what he's doing," the older man reassured her.

Chocky sidled along the ledge. "Susie says, no. Susie says, you'll be sorry. Sorrysorry. Sorrysorry. Allfalldown!"

A horrible premonition hit the three friends together and they all shouted at Alec.

"No, don't!"

"Come down!"

"Don't try to—"

Chocky gave a shrill screech, just like an old steam locomotive whistle. And the ladder, with Alec on it, juddered violently.

"Wha—" Alec started to say; then the word turned to a yell of disbelief and fright as the ladder tipped sideways and jerked away from the wall. It teetered, Alec lost his footing, tried to grab the ledge but missed.

"It's going – *aaaah!*" His voice went up in a wail, and the other men leaped for the ladder. "Get down!" the older one bawled, as the ladder seemed to fight them, jolting and jumping. "Slide – *quick!*"

Alec started to scramble down. He got half way when suddenly the ladder was snatched out of the men's hands. It came crashing down on top of them, and all three men fell in a tangle on the floor, while from the ledge Chocky – or Susie – screeched and hooted with delight.

Thankfully, the men weren't hurt. But they

were furious, and nothing Kel, Kate or Steve could say made any difference. "*Out!*" the foreman told them. Never mind the something bird, it could something well stay here till it starved to death for all he cared, and if he had any more trouble from something kids he'd belt the something lot of them himself. With his threats following them all the way to the door, the three fled. They didn't have any choice.

And Chocky was still loose in the hall.

"Oh God!" Kate leaned against the corridor wall and shut her eyes. "What're we going to do *now*?"

"We'll have to tell someone," said Steve dismally. "We can't leave things like this; Chocky's got to be caught before Susie does anything else."

Kate disagreed. "What's the point in telling anyone? They'll all know soon enough anyway."

"Yeah, and who's going to get the blame for letting him escape?" Kel added. "Us!"

"Well, we did, didn't we?" Kel glowered at Steve. "If you hadn't been such a prat—"

"Oh yeah? Who opened the cage door to start with?" Steve said indignantly.

"We had to!" Kate argued. "Poor Chocky was getting badly shaken – he'd have been hurt!"

"Oh, *great*! So now Susie's free to go around doing whatever she wants to anyone who gets in her way!"

"Chocky's got to eat," Kel pointed out. "He'll come for his food eventually; he'll have to."

"So what do we do till then?"

Kel was about to say that there wasn't much they could do, when the door to the hall opened and the workmen came out.

"You still here?" the foreman growled. "I thought I told you to vanish."

"We only—" Kate began, but he didn't let her finish.

"We're off home, and I'm not leaving you lot hanging around. Go on – out. *Now*."

"But Chocky—"

"I told you: the blasted bird can stay where it is. And you've got till I count three to get out of my sight. One. . ."

They went. The men followed them out of the building, and any thoughts they might have had about doubling back were foiled, because the foreman watched them all the way to the bus stop.

"Tomorrow morning—" Kate started to say.

"Don't." Kel didn't want to know about tomorrow morning. He didn't want to know about what they might find when they got to school, or what Mrs Dwyer and the Head were going to have to say about Chocky escaping. He just wanted to go home, stick his head under his duvet and tell himself that none of this was happening. It wouldn't really help. But at least he could pretend.

There was a feeling much worse than butter-flies in Kel's stomach as he walked up the school drive the next day. The building was still intact (which was something, he supposed) and there weren't any ambulances or police cars outside. But the peace didn't last for long because Mrs Dwyer knew that Chocky was loose, and she had a very good idea of who was responsible.

"Don't try to deny it, any of you!" she stormed at the three of them. "You were seen in the new wing after school hours, and it doesn't need a genius to work out what you were up to!" Kel, Kate and Steve could only listen as she banged on about stupidity, irresponsibility and anything else she could think of. Mrs Dwyer was convinced that they'd let Chocky out deliberately, to spite her, and their protests that it was an accident fell on deaf ears. Finally, at the end of the tirade, came the sting in the tail.

"You've got until the end of today to catch that bird," Mrs Dwyer told them. "I've spoken to the Head, and he agrees – if it's not back in its cage by then, it will be let out of the building, and good riddance!"

They were aghast. "You can't do that!" Kate protested. "Chocky wouldn't survive outside!"

"You should have thought of that before," said the teacher. "You've only got yourselves to blame. Now, get your books out. And I don't want to hear another word on the subject!"

As soon as the morning break bell rang, they went looking for Chocky.

They found him in the gym. He had roosted on the climbing frame – as the mess on the floor beneath proved. Now he was sidling up and down the top bar, crooning to himself and occasionally squawking "Atishoo!" or "Allfall-down!"

News of the escape had got round fast, and when Kel and his friends arrived, Chocky already had an audience. There were a dozen Year Fours and Fives, and about the same number of older students, including some of their own classmates. And, to their surprise and alarm, they found they were celebrities.

"That was brilliant, letting him out!"

"Mrs D's really got her knickers in a twist!"

"And the Shipwreck was having hysterics this morning!"

Kel rounded on them. "It isn't funny!" he said furiously. "If we can't catch him by the end of today, they're going to drive him out of the building, and then what'll happen to him?"

Faces fell. "They can't!" one of the younger kids said.

"Can't they? You just watch!"

"We ought to tell the RSPCA!"

"Yeah, fine; but by the time they can do any-thing – *if* they can – it'll be too late, won't it? We've got to catch him, that's all. So instead of standing around like a load of dummies, why don't you help us?"

To give them their credit, Kel grudgingly admitted later, once they'd seen the sense in what he was saying they all tried. But in a lot of ways, having helpers only made things worse. All through the morning and afternoon breaks, and the lunch hour, the school was in chaos as more and more people heard the story and joined in the efforts to catch Chocky. There seemed to be running, shouting figures everywhere; even some of the teachers joined in when they realized they couldn't stop the tide.

But they didn't stand a chance. Being chased by a noisy crowd only made Chocky more and more agitated. The crowd got over-excited, too – it should have been easy to trap Chocky in one room, but every time someone tried, someone else spoiled it. Yells of "Shut that door! Oh, no, he's out again!" rang down the corridors, and Chocky flapped and fluttered all over the school, screeching and squawking and "Atishoo"-ing. Sometimes he'd scream in Susie's voice: *"Susie says NO! Spitbellybum-drawers! Allfalldown!"* and whenever he did that, there was an accident – people slipped over or crashed into each other and bruised themselves; or someone knocked something flying and smashed it. And two windows got broken without anyone being anywhere near them.

Susie was working herself into a frenzy. And by the end of the day, Chocky was still on the loose.

It wouldn't have been so bad, Kel thought later, if Chocky had hidden himself somewhere by the time school was over. That way, at least there'd have been a chance of his still being in the building the next day. But fate wasn't feeling friendly, and at four o'clock the mynah bird was flapping and squawking by one of the side doors.

They made one last attempt to plead with Mrs Dwyer, but it was hopeless. The teacher's expression was nothing short of triumphant as she slammed up the bar and let the door swing open. Chocky, who had landed on the top hinge, peered at the world outside. Then he looked at Kel.

"Susie says, *boo*!" He blew an enormous raspberry, raised his tail and deposited a dollop of bird-lime on the floor. Then he launched himself from his perch, and flew like an arrow, out of the school and away.

For two or three seconds Kel stood frozen, staring numbly after the diminishing dark speck that was Chocky. He was so tired and miserable and confused that he didn't know what he thought any more: part of him was furious, part desperately worried, another part even relieved. Susie had been a menace. She'd been dangerous.

But Chocky was still Chocky, wasn't he? None of this was his fault. He was as much Susie's victim as anyone she'd attacked. It wasn't fair to abandon him. It just wasn't *fair*.

The anger and the worry suddenly overcame everything else. Kel didn't look at Mrs Dwyer and he didn't wait for Kate or Steve. He just dived through the door, and started to run in the direction that Chocky had taken.

# 10

"Kel, wait for us!"

Kel heard Steve and Kate shouting, and heard their pounding footsteps behind him, but he didn't slow down. Only when he came to a road and had to stop for the traffic did he pause and allow them to catch up.

"It's all right – for you!" Kate panted as she slithered to a halt. "You're a – faster runner than us!"

Kel didn't look at her; he was searching the sky beyond the road and the houses on the far side. The black, flying speck had vanished, but he'd marked where Chocky was heading, and

102

he pointed to where a stone tower showed through the trees.

"He's gone towards that church."

"St Peter's?" Kate narrowed her eyes to look. "I can't see any sign of him."

"Neither can I, now. But that's where he went." Kel looked to left and right; the road was clear. "Come on!"

They ran through a small housing estate, and within a few minutes the church was in sight. The Victorian building looked out of place; new houses crowded almost to the surrounding wall, and the little green patch of the churchyard was like an oasis in a desert.

"Yecch." Steve said as they went in at the lych-gate. "Gravestones. They give me the creeps."

"People don't get buried here now," Kate told him. "They stopped using it years ago. There probably isn't even a vicar any more."

"Great! So all the bodies have been rotting under there for centuries," Steve grumbled. "That's supposed to make me feel better, is it? What did they all die of – the plague?"

"Don't be so stupid! Anyway, you don't have to look at the gravestones; it's Chocky we want to find."

As Kate said it, Kel saw the mynah bird. Chocky was sitting in a yew tree on the far side of the churchyard. He was hard to see against the dark green leaves, but his orange beak gave him away, and Kel nudged the others.

"There – look!"

Cautiously, they started to move towards the tree. They hoped Chocky hadn't noticed them, but when they were still fifteen or twenty metres away, the mynah bird cocked his head and looked straight at them. Then he opened his wings and flapped off the branch.

"Blast!" said Kate. "He's gone!"

"No, hang on." Kel pointed. "He's landing again. There, on that gravestone; see him?"

The stone was the last one of a short row of stones half hidden in long grass and weeds. Perching on the top of it, Chocky bobbed up and down, then gave his loud, clear train-whistle.

"Maybe Susie can't control him out here?" Steve suggested hopefully. "Maybe she can only get to him when he's in the school?"

That hadn't occurred to Kel, and hope rose. "If she's not around, he'll be easier to catch," he said. "He knows us. And I've got a chocolate biscuit in my pocket."

"Go on, then," said Kate. "Try him with it."

Moving very slowly, Kel advanced on Chocky, holding out the biscuit. "Hi, Chocky," he said gently. "Chocky biscuit? Come on, boy."

Chocky eyed the biscuit greedily, and for a blissful moment Kel really thought he'd take the bait. He was only three steps away – almost within grabbing distance – when suddenly Chocky gave a harsh screech and flew up into the air.

*"Susie says, no! Atishoo, atishoo, Susie says atishoo! Allfalldown! Allfalldown!"*

"Oh, no!" Kate groaned despairingly. "She's still here!"

Susie was, and with a vengeance. Chocky seemed to go crazy, flapping and fluttering in an incredible mid-air dance and screaming in Susie's voice. Most of what he screamed made no sense; the only recognizable words were "Atishoo", "Allfalldown" and "Bless Susie", which he repeated over and over again. Finally he all but hurled himself on to another tree branch, too high for them to reach, and sat there, wings half open, staring down at them.

"Susie says, Atishoo! Susie says, Bless you! Bless Susie. Bless Susie. Bless school . . . Allfalldown."

Kel frowned. There was something weird about this; Chocky's tone had changed suddenly from squalling fury to something that sounded sad, almost pathetic.

"Susie?" He took a tentative step towards the tree. "It's all right, Susie. We don't want to hurt you."

"Bless Susie . . . Allfalldown. . ." said Chocky.

"All right." Kel nodded. "Bless Susie. But why? What are you trying to tell us?"

For a few moments Chocky gazed at him. Then he uttered one last "Atishoo!" and launched himself from the branch, flying swiftly away and vanishing beyond the trees.

They stared after him until he was out of sight, then with a sigh Kate leaned against the gravestone.

"That's it. We'll never be able to follow him now."

The boys said nothing; there was nothing to say. Disconsolately Kel scraped with one foot at the moss on the gravestone where Chocky had perched. There were several names on the stone; the first one, he noticed, was Alfred William Merry, but that didn't tell him anything and he stopped scraping and turned away. There didn't seem any point in hanging around, so they trudged back to the gate, out of the churchyard and towards the bus stop.

"We could put up some posters," Steve said after a while. "You know: 'Lost bird - reward' or something."

"Yeah," Kel's voice was flat.

"Well, it might work. It's about the only chance we've got of ever seeing him again."

"Shut up, Steve," said Kate. "You're only making us feel worse." She glanced at Kel, sympathy in her eyes. "It wasn't your fault, Kel. If you want to blame someone, blame Susie. Whoever she is – or was."

Kel nodded. He didn't speak, but Kate's words set him thinking. Just for a moment, as Chocky sat in that tree, he had almost felt that Susie really was listening to him, and that she wanted to make herself understood. So maybe they *could* find a way to talk to her. The paper letters idea had backfired badly, but—

Kel stopped walking suddenly as realization

hit him like a thunderbolt. Of course – of *course!* *That* was why the letters had made Susie so angry!

"Kel?" Kate had stopped too and was peering at him curiously. "What's up?"

"I've thought of something," Kel said. "Something about Susie." He swung to face them. "When we tried those cut-out letters—"

"Don't remind me!" Kate groaned.

"*Listen.* It got her mad, right? And you know why? Because she didn't know how to use them. She can't read or write!"

Kate and Steve stared at him blankly, but before they could ask any questions, he rushed on. "Think about the way Susie's voice sounds. And the things she says. Nursery rhymes, stupid poems; it's all little kids' stuff! *So how old is Susie?*"

Kate's mouth dropped open. "Oh my God. . . It was staring us in the face, and we never saw it! She *is* just a little kid! Probably no more than six or seven!"

"And little kids throw tantrums, don't they?"

"Yes!" Kate had two small brothers, and knew exactly what he meant. "We've got to talk to her in a way she can understand!"

"Fine," said Steve. "But that's only going to make it more difficult, isn't it? How can we make her stop this if she only knows goo-goo and ga-ga?"

"Don't be a prat; she's not *that* babyish," Kate told him scornfully. "Look, I'm going home, and I'm going to think about this and make some plans."

"You've forgotten something," Steve pointed out. "Susie talks through Chocky. And Chocky's gone."

"That's right; cheer us up, why don't you?" Kate said sourly. "We *know* Chocky's gone. But Susie wants something. She's made that pretty obvious."

"So," Kel finished, seeing that Steve still hadn't grasped it, "chances are that Chocky'll be back. Sooner or later."

"And I reckon," said Kate, "that it'll be sooner."

That night, Kel slept a restless sleep filled with unpleasant dreams. In most of them he was wandering through gloomy, twilit rooms. There were lights, but they didn't work when he pressed any of the switches. And wherever he went, a childish little voice seemed to float after him, saying over and over again, "*Bless Susie . . . bless Susie. . .*" then giggling horribly. He heard Chocky's shrill train-whistle again, only this time it turned into the sound of a loud, harsh bell that jangled on and on and wouldn't stop. Then, just as he thought his eardrums were going to burst with the din of it, he woke up with a jolt.

And from outside his bedroom window, very softly, came a little voice: "*Susie says, bless you. . .*"

Kel was at the window in less than three seconds. But there was nothing outside. At least, nothing that he could see. . .

He didn't get back to sleep again. He didn't want to; that last dream had been more than enough. Instead, he lay awake thinking. Planning.

And wondering. Wondering how all this had started. What had made Susie come back to haunt them. What she really wanted.

And what might happen if she didn't get it. . .

# 11

No one knew how he could possibly have done it, but Chocky was back in the school building the next morning.

Kel, Steve and Kate heard about it the moment they walked in at the main door. In an instant they were surrounded by a horde of their schoolmates, all talking at once. It took a while to make any sense of the story, but eventually they unravelled it. It seemed that the school secretary had come in early to look over the exhibition set out in the new hall. She was unlocking the outside door when there was a whirr of wings and Chocky fluttered out of the sky and landed on her shoulder. The secretary wasn't the kind of person to be fazed by anything, so she quickly went inside, shut the door and tried to grasp hold of him. Chocky, though, wasn't having any of that. He instantly flew off, and now he was loose in the school again.

"He's got into the hall now," someone said. "We tried to go and see, but the Head's there and he won't let us in."

The three looked at each other, all thinking the same thing.

"We can try. . ." said Kate.

They headed for the hall. There was quite a crowd outside, too many for them to see what was going on beyond the glass door panels.

" 'Scuse us," said Kel, barging past. There were protests, but they pushed their way through and, before anyone could stop them, went in.

The Head, the Deputy Head and the school secretary were in the hall. They were all staring up towards the high ceiling, but at the sound of the door the Head looked round.

"I told you to stay out!" he snapped. "Go on – back outside!"

"Just a minute, Mr Wright," the secretary said. "These three look after Chocky, don't they? He knows them, so he might be more likely to come down to them."

From up above them, faintly, came a squawk of: "A-TISH-oo!"

The Head frowned. "Well. . ."

"Please, Mr Wright!" Kate entreated. "Let us try!"

"Oh . . . all right, then. But not now." The Head nodded up at the roof. "The bird's excited; it needs time to calm down. I'll lock the door so it can't get out, and you can come back at break and see what you can do. But just you three, mind. No one else."

*No way do we want anyone else!* Kel thought. "Thanks, Mr Wright!"

Chocky called down, "Susie says, *boo!*" and the secretary smiled. "He's very talkative, isn't he?" she commented. "It was quite strange; when he landed on my shoulder this morning, he said, 'Susie says, Brrr!' Just as if he was trying to tell me he felt the cold. You'd almost think he really understands human speech."

*Yeah*, Kel thought, suppressing an unpleasant shiver, *you would, wouldn't you?*

*And you don't know how nearly right you are!*

He could feel Chocky – or Susie – watching them as they all walked towards the door. Once outside the Head told the crowd that this wasn't a circus and there was nothing to see, and reluctantly they started to disperse. The Deputy Head and the secretary went out, then the Head turned to wait for Kel, Steve and Kate.

"I want that bird caught," he said. "Today's Thursday, so you've got a bit of time before Saturday."

"Saturday?" said Kel blankly.

The Head gave him a long-suffering look. "Yes, Kelvin, Saturday. Don't you *ever* listen to what I say in assembly?"

It clicked. Saturday – the opening day of the new block!

"Oh, no. . ." Kel hissed.

"Exactly," said the Head. "And the last thing we want, with parents, governors, the vicar and half the town council here, is that mynah bird disrupting everything and causing havoc. So I want an all-out effort; and if you need any help, come straight to me. Understand?"

They nodded pallidly. "Right. . ."

"Good." Satisfied that he'd drummed it into them, the Head walked out of the hall. Kel and his friends were about to follow when, from his high perch, Chocky squawked again.

"Susie says, Atishoo! Susie says, Bless you!" A pause. "Bless you, bless Susie, bless school! *New* school!"

And an evilly malevolent giggle echoed down from the rafters.

"Hurry up, you three; I haven't got all day," the Head called. Either he hadn't heard what Chocky said, or he hadn't seen anything significant in it. But Kel had. Suddenly, horribly, something had slipped into place.

Bless school – *new* school. On Saturday, at the opening ceremony, the vicar was going to bless the new block.

And Kel knew with an awful certainty that Susie was planning to make trouble.

*Big* trouble. Bigger than they could begin to guess. . .

Their first efforts to catch Chocky were a hopeless failure. He simply stayed out of reach, and no amount of cajoling or bribery with chocolate biscuits made any difference. It was almost as if Susie was taunting them, Kel thought; and the more wound up they became, the more she enjoyed it. Chocky dashed and darted around the hall, squawking and chuckling and giggling, and volleys of "Susie says, *boo!*" and "Allfalldown!" rang out until the three of them could have screamed.

At lunchtime they tried again – only this time with a difference. The school secretary had come to their rescue, and found a large piece of netting in an old cupboard. Nobody knew what it had once been used for, but it was just what they needed now.

"Right," said Kel determinedly as they entered the hall and shut the door behind them. "Let's see what he makes of *this*."

Their idea was that he and Steve should position themselves with the net spread out between them, and Kate would try to drive Chocky into it. The exhibition stuff was a bit of a nuisance, because they had to be careful not to knock things over and there wasn't much space to manoeuvre. At the moment Chocky was perching on a large wooden plaque that had been put up on the wall. It was covered with a cloth, and would be officially unveiled on opening day; it had something to do with the school's history, but Kel didn't know what it said, and wasn't interested now. He tensed as Kate started to tiptoe towards the mynah bird. Chocky eyed her cautiously, whistled, then announced, "Susie's here. . ."

"We know," said Kate. "Come on, Susie, please. Let Chocky come to us. We won't hurt him, and we won't hurt you."

Steve smothered a snort. "Some chance!"

"Shh!" Kel glowered at him. "She'll hear!"

Steve shrugged. "So what? She's not going to fall for this anyway. *I* think—"

They never did find out what he thought, because at that moment Chocky launched himself away from his perch. With a shock Kel realized that he was flying straight towards them – straight at the net!

"*Steve!*" he yelled.

They jumped together, holding the net as high as they could reach – and Chocky flew right into it. There was a raucous screech, and Kel, Steve and the net, with Chocky tangled in its folds, all collided together.

"*Susie says no, NO!*" The childish voice was filled with rage as Chocky beat his wings furiously, trying to break free. Then Kate shouted, "Look OUT!" and the boys spun round in time to see an object spinning through the air towards them. Kel had one instant to register the fact that the object was a large map on a hardboard backing, then he ducked, and the map whizzed over his head with only centimetres to spare.

"*Spitbellybumdrawers!*" shrieked Chocky. "*Susie says BOO, BOO, BOO!*"

Kate yelled another warning as a second picture tore itself free from the wall and hurtled across the hall. A chair, which was part of a display showing how a classroom had looked years ago, started to dance and jiggle. Then came a noise like thunder, as a long trestle table suddenly and violently tipped sideways, sending a collection of old school registers crashing to the floor.

"Susie!" Kel shouted. "Stop it!"

Chocky screeched anew. The spotlights started to shake on their fixings, a bulb exploded, showering glass all over the place, and another table collapsed with a grating groan.

"Get Chocky out!" Frantically Kel dived among the folds of the net, struggling to untangle the mynah bird. If he escaped again, if they could never catch him, it didn't matter – they had to make Susie stop!

Kate was twisting and turning, trying to field flying objects and falling tables. Kel glimpsed her wading into the classroom display, where an old-time desk was shaking as though in an earthquake. As Kate made a grab for it, the desk jumped a metre off the floor – then it twisted in mid-air, and before Kate could dodge, the heavy wooden base thwacked her full in the midriff.

"*Ufff!*" Kate went down like a skittle. And as she slumped to the floor, the mayhem stopped. It didn't just die away – it stopped, completely and instantaneously. Stillness and silence crashed into the hall, and for a moment the boys stood gaping like stranded fish, too shocked to react. Then the paralysis snapped and, forgetting Chocky, they ran to help Kate.

She wasn't hurt, only winded. The desk lay on its side, and as they hauled Kate to her feet Steve gave it a revengeful kick. The desk juddered and the lid dropped open. And Kate, who was nearer to its level than the boys were, froze.

"*Look. . .*" She hadn't got her breath back yet and her voice was a hoarse whisper. One hand pointed shakily to the underside of the desk lid.

There was something scratched there. Letters. The desk was very old, and among all the gouges and stains the carved words were hard to read. But when they looked closer, they were able to make them out.

The letters spelled a name, and a date. In clumsy capitals, as if whoever scratched them was only just learning to write, they said:

## SUSIE MERRY 1918.

As the three stared in astonishment at the letters, a sad little chirp sounded behind them. The childish voice muffled by the folds of the net, Chocky said, very quietly, "Atishoo, atishoo, all fall down. . ."

It seemed they had found Susie.

# 12

"I don't think they go that far back," Steve said.

"They've got to! Keep looking." Kel picked up another armful of books and papers and dumped them on the trestle table. Kate was searching through a third pile, but so far they hadn't had any luck.

It had been Kate's idea to check Susie Merry's name against the old school records on display, but so far the earliest ones they could find were from the 1930s. The trouble was, Susie's furious outburst had made an almighty mess of the exhibition, and now everything was out of order. They'd have to straighten it all up as best they could, but this was more important.

A short way off, Chocky sat watching their activity. When the uproar suddenly stopped, he too had calmed down, and it had been the easiest thing in the world to untangle him from the net and pop him back in his cage. Since then he hadn't uttered a sound, but Kel had the feeling that Susie was still there. Something else was nagging at him, too. The surname: Merry. He'd come across it before somewhere. Were there any Merrys in the school now? No, he thought, it wasn't that. But he *had* seen that name before.

Suddenly Steve said, "Hey, I think this is it!"

"Where?" Kel and Kate ran to look, and Kel clenched his fist. "1918 – yeah! You've found it!"

The register was a big cloth-bound ledger, its pages yellow with age. They started to thumb through it, and after a minute Kate said, "Here – Merry, look!"

"Wrong Merry," Kel said. "That one's Grace Ethel."

"And there's another one," said Steve,

pointing. "Alfred William. And there – John George."

"There's loads of them," Kate added. She was tracing down the columns in the book. "Bertha Elizabeth, Stanley Arthur, Frederick Charles, Mary Phyllis – *ah*! Susan Martha! That's her, it's got to be!"

There it was near the bottom of the page: Susan Martha Merry. She must have been the youngest of all those brothers and sisters, they decided. But what had happened to her?

Steve turned over more pages. Each term, when the list of pupils was entered in the book, the Merrys appeared.

Until suddenly they weren't there any more.

"They've all gone," said Kate wonderingly. "Every one of them."

"And so have a lot of other names," Kel pointed out. "There's only about half the number here."

Kate looked very thoughtful for a few moments. Then she said, "What year have we got to?"

Steve checked. "1919," he said. "Why?"

"Oh my God . . . don't you remember what we did in history last year? About the First

World War, and what happened afterwards?"

History wasn't Kel's favourite subject, but abruptly a memory crept back. "The 'flu epidemic of 1919. . ." he whispered.

"Yes. Mr Levine said more people died of the 'flu than were killed in the whole war."

Then from the direction of Chocky's cage came a small voice: "Atishoo . . . atishoo . . . we all fall down. . ."

And a memory slammed into Kel's mind.

"The churchyard!" he almost shouted. "When we chased Chocky there, you remember? He perched on a gravestone – there were lots of names on it; I didn't bother to read them all, but I saw one." He swallowed. "Alfred William Merry."

"And there's an Alfred William in the book. . ." whispered Kate. She and Steve raised their gaze from the register and stared at Kel. "*All* the Merrys died?" Steve said softly.

"It looks like it, doesn't it?" said Kel grimly.

Kate shuddered. "That's what Susie was trying to tell us, with all those 'atishoos'. It wasn't 'Ring a ring of roses'. It was the 'flu." She turned and moved slowly towards Chocky's cage. "Oh, Susie . . . I'm so sorry for you!"

Chocky looked back at her with his bright bird eyes, but he didn't say anything else.

"But why has she come back?" Kel asked. "That's what I don't understand. Why her, and none of the others?" He frowned. "And why *now*?"

"That's the mystery we've got to solve, isn't it?" Kate gazed thoughtfully at Chocky again, then crouched down in front of the cage. "Why *are* you here, Susie?" she asked.

"Atishoo," Chocky replied. "Bless Susie. Atishoo."

"She isn't going to tell us," said Steve.

"Maybe there's a clue on that gravestone," Kel suggested. "I think we should go back there and look."

Kate shook her head. "It won't say much, though we ought to check all the names, to make sure we're right." She concentrated on Chocky again. "Susie. . . we think we know what happened to you, but we can't help unless you can tell us what you want."

An odd little chuckling sound came from Chocky's throat. Then he started to sing: "London's burning, London's burning; fetch the engine, fetch the engine! Fire, fire! Fire, fire!"

The song stopped abruptly. Chocky said: "Bless school. *New* school." There was an ugly emphasis on the word "new". And then, in a childish but very unpleasant way, he giggled.

And Kel realized to his horror what Susie was planning.

"She's going to start a fire. . ." he whispered, aghast. "The new block – she's going to try and burn it down!"

"She can't!" Kate whirled to face him. "She hasn't got that sort of power!"

"Want to bet?" Kel's face was white, and he felt sick. "Think what she's already done!" In three strides he was at the cage and he grasped hold of it. "Susie! You mustn't do this – you *mustn't*!"

"Spitbellybumdrawers!" said Chocky. "London's burning, London's burning; Susie says, London's burning!"

"*Listen* to us, Susie!" Kate pleaded.

But Chocky was getting excited, and he started to squawk at the top of his voice. "*Susie says, boo! Atishoo, atishoo, we all fall down! Bless Susie, bless Susie, everybody bless Susie! London's burning, fetch the engine, SusieSusieSusieSusie!*"

"Where's all this racket coming from?" a new voice cut in loudly from the door. "What's going on in here?"

It was the Head. He strode towards them, taking in the scene with a sweeping look. "Good God, this hall looks as if a bomb's hit it! What on earth have you been *doing*?"

"We've caught Chocky, Mr Wright," Kel said helplessly.

The Head glowered at the cage. "Well, I suppose that's something to be thankful for. But this time he'd better *stay* caught!" He marched to the cage and picked it up. "I'll take him back to the activity room, which will then be locked."

"But Mr Wright, he'll need feeding—"

"The caretaker will see to that. You three aren't going near him! As for what you *are* going to do. . ." The Head's mouth hardened. "You've got an hour to get the hall straight again, or there'll be trouble!"

They tried to argue, but the Head wouldn't listen. The problem was, they couldn't tell him why it was so vital for them to have access to Chocky. They couldn't tell him about Susie. He simply wouldn't have believed a word of it.

The Head stomped out, carrying Chocky in his cage. Fading away down the corridor, they heard Chocky singing in Susie's voice.

"Fire, fire! Fire, fire! Bless school. *New* school. . ."

"It's the opening day on Saturday," Steve said in a hollow, frightened voice. "Do you think. . .?"

Kel and Kate both nodded. "It's obvious, isn't it?" said Kate. "Too good a chance for Susie to miss." She swallowed. "We can't warn anybody. And we can't take Chocky away from the school; we can't even *get* to him now. Oh God – what are we going to do?"

The trouble was, none of them had an answer.

And they had less than forty-eight hours to come up with one.

# 13

They tried everything they could think of to get into the activity room, but they failed. There was no way they could get to Chocky again until Saturday. By which time, Kel thought miserably, it might be far too late.

The only hope they had now was the gravestone, and as soon as school was over they ran back to the little churchyard in the housing estate. But their hopes collapsed when they found the stone again. It was the Merry children's grave, all right; but it told them only what they had already guessed for themselves.

Tragically, the Merrys had all died of the 'flu

within a few days of one another. And the final name on the stone, nearly hidden in the overgrown grass, was "Susan Martha, aged 6 years".

"Only six," Kate said in a soft, shocked voice. "Oh, the poor little kid!" She was nearly in tears. Steve, though, was cynical.

"Don't start feeling sorry for her. She's not an ordinary kid; she's a dangerous menace!"

Kel didn't comment. He could see both Kate and Steve's points of view, and didn't know which one he agreed with. Sitting on the bus, and later at home, all he knew was that he was tangled in a nightmare of worrying. It was almost as if Susie was in his head, haunting him, and the four awful questions of *what*, *when*, *how* and *why* hammered in his brain. In his room, he even tried shutting his eyes tightly and trying to make telepathic contact with Susie. It didn't work, of course. It probably wouldn't even have worked with Chocky around. Susie was determined, and no amount of pleading was going to stop her.

The other thing that didn't work was his attempt on Friday evening to persuade his parents not to go to the opening ceremony.

"Don't be ridiculous, Kel!" Dad said. "Of course Mum and I are going! And you ought to have some pride in your school, instead of moaning because you've got to give up just one Saturday. It's not exactly asking the earth of you, is it?"

"Unless there's something you don't want us to find out about, of course," Mum chipped in suspiciously. "Is that it? Have you done something at school that you're ashamed of?"

"No!" Kel protested. "It's just that . . . well, it's going to be really boring. Just a load of speeches and stuff. And the new block isn't worth looking at."

"It is to us," Dad said firmly. "So we're going tomorrow, all of us, and that's flat. Now get on with your tea."

But Kel couldn't eat. When he went to bed he couldn't sleep either, and when he did finally doze off, he had a string of nightmares about himself and all his family and friends being trapped and burned to death in the blazing school. At six o'clock he woke up in a sweat of terror, and after that he lay tense and miserable, trying not to think about anything at all, until at last he had no choice but to get up and face the dreaded day.

Dad drove them to the school. By the time they got there the car park was nearly full, and a black limo with the town crest on it showed that the mayor's party had already arrived. Kel's parents wanted to look around before the ceremonies started, so Kel took his chance and ran off in search of Kate and Steve.

He found Kate in the gym, her twin toddler brothers in tow.

"I've got to look after them," she said distractedly. "I tried everything I could think of to get out of it, but Mum insisted. So I daren't do anything."

"Oh hell!" Kel glared at the twins, who scowled sulkily back. "Does Steve know?"

"Yeah; I saw him a few minutes ago. He's gone to see if he can get to Chocky."

"I'd better find him."

"Come back and tell me what's happening!" Kate pleaded.

Kel waved acknowledgement and hurried out.

To his enormous relief, the activity room had been unlocked. Steve was in there, but so were a lot of other people. In fact there was quite a crowd around Chocky's cage, and Chocky sat crooning and preening, thoroughly enjoying all the attention.

"He's not talking much," Steve told Kel. "And there's no sign of Susie – so far, anyway."

That didn't mean she wasn't there; but with so many people about, any thoughts they might have had about trying to reason with her went straight out of the window.

"We'll just have to hang around and hope for a chance to get Chocky on his own," Kel said.

"We could take it in turns," Steve suggested. "That way, it won't look so suspicious." He frowned. "It's a real pain about Kate – we could have done with her, too."

"Maybe she'll be able to get away later. Look, you take the first turn here. I'll tell Kate what we're doing, keep my folks happy for half an hour or so, then come back and relieve you."

"OK," said Steve. Then a worried look crept over his face. "But what if something . . . *happens?*"

Kel hesitated, thinking. Then he said, "I don't know. I honestly don't."

\* \* \*

For more than an hour nothing did happen. In one way that was an enormous relief; in another, though, Kel found himself wishing that Susie would just get on and do whatever she was planning. At least then they'd know what they were up against, and however bad it was, it would surely be better than this agony of suspense.

Even without Kate to help them, he and Steve had managed to keep a close eye on Chocky. The official opening ceremony had now finished. They'd heard the drone of speeches from the assembly hall, the vicar's blessing, and applause as the new plaque, whatever it was, had been unveiled by the mayor. While all that was going on they'd had a chance to tackle Susie – but whatever they tried, whatever they said, Susie wasn't answering them. Chocky just sat on his perch and looked cute, and he wouldn't say a word.

Both boys were in the activity room, trying again and failing again to get through to Susie, when they heard the shuffle of a lot of feet in the distance.

"What on earth. . .?" Kel frowned.

Steve stuck his head out of the door, then hastily ducked back in again.

"It's the Head's guided tour for the big noises and parents!" he said. "They're at the end of the corridor, and it looks like they're heading this way!"

"Oh, *no*!" If the Head found them, he'd get suspicious and throw them out. "Quick," Kel said. "Let's shift before they see us. We'll go round the long way, tag on the end of the procession, then drop back in here again when they've done this room. We might get a chance to see Kate, too."

They sneaked out of the activity room and dodged into a side passage that would bring them round behind the tour party. After they had vanished, Chocky looked at the door for a few moments. He seemed to be thinking.

Then, with a disturbing note of gleeful satisfaction, he said: "A. . .TISH. . .oo. . ."

Kel and Steve found Kate near the back of the crowd, still towing along her little brothers, who were getting bored and grizzly by this time. She flicked a warning glance towards the

135

backs of her parents just ahead, then hissed, "Anything happened?"

"No," said Kel. "There's still no sign of Susie. It's all quiet so far."

"*Too* quiet, if you ask me," Steve added ominously.

Kel ignored him. "We're going back to the activity room once this lot's been in there and gawped at everything. Can you get away and join us?"

"Not a chance." Kate shook her head. "Mum's got talking to the Shipwreck, of all people, so she won't want these two round her neck. And Dad's a complete male chauvinist pig; he thinks looking after them's a woman's job. So I'm stuck. But I should be able to get away after the tour stuff. I'll tell Mum I've got to do something for Mrs Dwyer, and I'll meet you in the activity room as soon as I can."

The procession moved slowly on. A lot of people wanted to look at a lot of things, and by the time the tail-enders had been into the activity room, the spearhead was already way down the corridor, where the Head was leading them into the new laboratory.

"Phew!" Steve let out a sigh of relief as the

last stragglers finally wandered out of the activity room, leaving them and Chocky alone. "I thought they'd never go."

Kel glanced at the cage. Chocky had uttered a few "Here we go"s and "Houston, we have lift-off"s for the visitors, but still there was no word from Susie. Was it possible, Kel asked himself hopefully, that they'd been wrong about her? Surely, *surely* if she was going to do anything they'd have seen the first signs by now?

Chocky said perkily: "Who's a pretty boy, then?"

Steve rolled his eyes. "They must have all been saying that to him! How corny can you get?"

"Corny!" repeated Chocky. "Corny boy!"

"Yeah, and you'll get a prize for it if you keep saying that," Steve told the bird. "Come on, say something better. Five - four - three—"

"Three-two-one!" Chocky finished it for him. "Three-two-one! Fire!"

Then he gave an evil giggle, and to their horror, Susie's high-pitched voice warbled from his throat.

"London's burning, London's burning; fetch the engine, fetch the engine. . ."

Icy hands clutched at Kel's gut. *"Susie!"*

"Fire, fire!" sang Chocky. "Fire, fire! Atishoo, atishoo, Susie says, atishoo! Bless Susie, bless school . . . *new* school!"

Realization hit Kel like a thunderbolt as he remembered where the guided tour had been heading. The lab – of *course!* It was the most howlingly obvious place of all: the place where a fire would be all too easy to start, and where the result could be hideously devastating!

"Steve!" He grabbed his friend's arm. "She's going to start a fire in the lab!"

*"What?"* Steve's eyes bulged. "How do you know?"

"I just *do!* Come on, for God's sake – we've got to warn them!"

Steve still didn't understand and might have started arguing. But as Kel tried to drag him towards the door, Chocky let out a raucous screech.

*"Too late, too late! Susie says, too late!"*

Steve's jaw dropped. Then he and Kel dived for the door together. They pounded along the corridor, swerved round the corner, and there were the lab doors ahead of them. They stood half open, and inside they could see a crowd of people gathered round the Head, who was showing off some of the new equipment.

Kel drew as much breath as he could spare. "Mr Wright!" he yelled. "Mr *Wright!*"

A burst of laughter from the visitors drowned his shout and no one heard him. No one was even looking; they didn't realize, couldn't see. . .

They were less than six strides from the lab doors when from the activity room they heard Chocky's distant shriek: "*TOO LATE!*" There was such murderous delight in the voice that the shock of it made Kel stumble. Recovering, he hurled himself after Steve, who had over-taken him. Three more paces, two, one. . .

And with no hand to touch them, the lab doors swung violently together and slammed shut in their faces.

# 14

Kate didn't hear the doors slam. People were still laughing at one of the Head's excruciating jokes, and anyway she was having trouble with the twins, who were grabbing at everything within reach and making complete pests of themselves.

"Craig!" she hissed as one of the toddlers tried to get hold of a local councillor's wife's ankle chain. "Stop it, now, or I'll thump you!"

Jason, the other twin, started to wail that he wanted a wee-wee. He'd only just had one, so Kate raised a threatening hand and he shut up. In the couple of seconds that took, Craig had another snatch at the ankle-chain.

"*Craig*. I'm not telling you again!" Much more of this and she'd just walk out and leave them to it. It *isn't fair*, she grumbled silently; *Mum and Dad are always landing me with them, and I—*

The thought broke off as, from somewhere behind her, came a small noise of breaking glass.

Kate turned her head. She was only just in time to see it, and when she did, her eyes opened as wide as an owl's.

The glass front of one of the chemicals cupboards had cracked right across. There was no one anywhere near it, but even as Kate stared, several pieces of the glazing fell out and dropped to the floor with a tinkling sound.

And the bottles on the shelves were moving. *Susie. . .*

"Mum. . ." Kate started to edge her way through the crowd, dragging the twins with her. There was a choking, panicky feeling growing in her chest, and her voice came out as a croak. "Mum . . . Dad. . ."

One of the bottles had reached the edge of the shelf. It teetered, then it fell. Smashed. This time there was enough noise for people to notice, and several heads turned.

"Oh, dear!" said a loud voice. "Who knocked that over?"

Suddenly, Kate knew with an awful certainty what was happening, what Susie had planned. A colourless liquid was spreading out from the shards of the broken bottle. It didn't smell of anything. But it *steamed*.

And another bottle was rocking on the brink of the shelf.

Kate's terror erupted, and she screamed at the top of her voice: "Get out! Everybody get OUT of here!"

At the same moment, the second bottle went crashing to the floor.

Kel and Steve saw the sudden rush for safety, but there was nothing they could do to help. The first wave of people reached the doors, and hands grabbed and grappled, trying to wrench them open. But the doors wouldn't budge.

"Open them!" someone yelled from inside, their voice muffled through the glass and wood. "Hurry, *hurry*!"

"We can't!" Kel shouted back. "They're jammed!"

He and Steve threw themselves against the doors again, as they'd done a dozen times, but it was useless. An enormous force was holding the doors fast, and mere human strength wasn't enough to break it.

Then Steve cried, "Look! *Smoke!*"

A dense, foggy cloud was rising from the floor inside the lab, roiling around the agitated faces behind the door. "Phone the fire brigade!" Kel screamed at Steve, who seemed to be hypnotized by the sight. "Go on – *run!*"

Steve's racing footsteps pounded away, and Kel wrestled again with the door handle. In the lab more glass shattered, and someone yelped as though with shock. Smoke was starting to curl under the door now. It had a weird purple tinge, and suddenly Kel smelled a hideous stench, like rotten eggs mixed with something even worse.

"*Kel!*" A blurred figure pressed its face and hands to the other side of the door, and to his horror Kel saw that it was Kate. "Kel, she's smashing all the chemical bottles!" A fit of coughing doubled her up, and between spasms she spluttered, "It isn't fire – it's *fumes*!"

As if to add to her warning, a dark brown bottle went hurtling past Kate's head and exploded against the wall. The contents – whatever they were – burst into flames; someone quickly stamped the fire out, but people were *really* starting to scream now.

They rushed the door again, but still it wouldn't give. Then feet thudded in the corridor behind Kel, as a group of teachers and parents came running.

"Out of the way!" one of them bellowed. Kel was shoved aside as three burly men threw themselves against the doors, and others rushed outside to try to smash the windows. But the doors held fast and the windows wouldn't break – somehow Susie was holding them, and the rescuers couldn't reach the trapped people in the lab. As the chemicals combined into a deadly mixture, they were all being poisoned and choked, and by the time the fire brigade arrived, then, as Susie had so gleefully claimed, it would be too late!

Kel knew that there was only one hope. Frantically signalling to Kate – though he couldn't tell whether she understood – he turned and sprinted back along the corridor. Bursting into the activity room, he flung himself to his knees in front of Chocky's cage.

"*Susie!*" he yelled, tears of terror and frustration streaming down his face. "*Susie, stop it, you've got to stop it! Let them out!*"

Chocky went berserk. Screeching: "*Susie says, no!*" he launched himself from his perch and flew against the cage bars, beating his wings furiously. "*Susie says, NO! Bless Susie! Atishoo, atishoo, atishoo!*"

"*You've got to!*" Kel screamed. He wrenched the cage door open and made a grab for Chocky, as if he could shake some sanity into Susie. Chocky dodged – then before Kel could react, he flew free from the cage and, wings pumping powerfully, hurtled out of the room.

"No!" Kel cried. "Come back, come *back*!" He tore after the mynah bird, and was in time to see him swooping towards the hall. Barging past more people who were heading for the lab, Kel raced into the hall. Chocky was diving and plunging around the exhibition, but the instant he saw Kel he changed course and headed straight for the newly unveiled plaque on the wall. Landing on its top edge, he started to bounce dementedly up and down, and his screech dinned in Kel's ears: "*Bless Susie, bless Susie, bless Susie!*"

And a single word at the top of the plaque snatched Kel's attention.

*EPIDEMIC*. . .

He hadn't realized before. He hadn't seen the plaque properly: until today it had been covered with a cloth, and he hadn't been in the hall when it was unveiled. But now he saw with a lurch of shock that it was a memorial. A memorial to all the children of this school who had died in the 1919 'flu epidemic!

Kel dashed towards the plaque. Chocky was still bouncing and screeching, "*Bless Susie, bless Susie!*" and Kel's gaze seared over the list of names on the board, looking for Susie Merry.

She wasn't there. A mistake had been made, and Susie had been left off the memorial list!

With blinding understanding, Kel realized why Susie had come back. *Bless Susie* – she wanted her name to be among the others. She wanted her blessing. . .

From outside came a rising wail of sirens and the squeal of tyres. But Kel knew that this was not something the fire brigade could deal with. Susie had to have what she wanted – and he was the only one who could give it to her in time!

He spun round, his eyes frantically searching. There – a visitor's book, and beside it a felt-tipped pen. Snatching the pen, Kel dragged a chair under the plaque and scrambled up.

"*Bless Susie!*" Chocky shrieked. "*Atishoo, atishoo!*"

There was just enough room to do it. Hand shaking, breath sawing in his throat, Kel wrote three words at the bottom of the list:

## SUSAN MARTHA MERRY

As he finished the last letter, the sound of splintering wood rang down the corridor, echoed by shouts of triumph. The rescuers had broken into the lab. Fire and ambulance sirens shrieked to a crescendo and stopped, and more feet thundered as voices began to bark out instructions.

Dizzy with fright and shock and relief and

fury all mingled together, Kel climbed down from the chair, then found he was too shaky to move any further. Chocky was silent, and for several seconds Kel could only stare blankly at the open hall door and the figures rushing past outside.

Until one figure saw him, stopped and came slowly in.

"Kel. . .?" said Steve.

"Are they . . . are they out?" Kel asked in a whisper.

"They're bringing them out now. Looks as if they're going to be all right."

Kel nodded. Then his legs gave way, and he slumped down on to the chair, utterly exhausted.

# 15

They stood dazedly in the hall doorway, watching as the last of the trapped people were brought out of the lab. The victims were coughing and gasping, but most of them could walk with someone helping them. Only two were on stretchers, and a kindly paramedic assured the boys as he hurried past that they'd soon be on their feet again.

Kate and her family had already been taken to one of the waiting ambulances. Kate had managed a watery smile as she passed, but hadn't been able to speak. Now firemen in breathing apparatus were going in to clean up the wreckage in the lab, and one of them gently shooed the boys back.

"Outside now, lads," he said. "We want everyone out of the building until this lot's been made safe."

Steve put a hand under Kel's elbow to steady him as they made their way towards the exit. In a few dazed sentences Kel had told his story, and they were both soberly silent as they thought of how nearly this had ended in tragedy. They'd forgotten about Chocky. But as they approached the outside doors, there was a whirr of wings and the mynah bird appeared, swooping towards them. Chocky landed on Kel's shoulder and, gently enough not to hurt, nibbled his ear. It was one of his favourite tricks, but he hadn't done it at all since Susie had come on the scene.

Then, in a cajoling little voice, he said: "Susie says, sorry. . ."

Kel felt sick. "*Sorry?*" he hissed savagely. "Sorry's not enough, is it? You could have *killed* them all!"

There was a strange, thoughtful expression on Steve's face, and suddenly he reached out and stroked Chocky's head. "Kel. . ." he said gently, "she was only six. Think about it. At that age they don't know any better, do they?"

On the verge of a furious reply, Kel paused. Steve was right, wasn't he? To a kid of six, the whole world revolved around them and no one else. They were selfish and couldn't help it. The only thing that had mattered to Susie was having her name on that plaque. Having her blessing. It was all she could think about, and she was too young to understand what her obsession might do to other people. As Steve said, she didn't know any better.

And no one had died. No one was even badly hurt. So couldn't he forgive Susie for what she'd done. . .?

He sighed wearily, and said in a kinder voice, "All right, Susie. I can't hate you; it wouldn't be fair. We'll get your name written properly on the plaque, then people won't forget you."

There was a pause. Then Chocky chirped softly: "Susie says, promise?"

"Promise." The Head would agree to it, Kel thought. He wouldn't want the plaque to be incomplete, and all they had to do was show him the old school records, with Susie's name in them. Maybe the vicar would even bless the plaque a second time. Bless Susie... Yes, they'd keep their promise to her. But neither Kel nor Steve nor Kate would ever tell anyone else this story. Susie would be remembered. But not for the disaster she had so nearly caused today. Really, truly, that *wouldn't* be fair.

Chocky had tucked his beak into his chest feathers and seemed to be falling asleep.

"We'll ask the firemen if we can get his cage, shall we?" said Steve.

"Yeah. I think he'll go back in it now."

Chocky opened his eyes again. Raising his head, he looked steadily at the boys for a moment. Then, very softly, he said: "Susie says, Bye-bye. . ."

Kel and Steve stared back at him. Chocky blinked beadily. Then in a voice that sounded just like Kel's, he announced: "Here we go, here we go, here we go! Three-two-one – Houston, we have lift-off!"

Despite everything, Kel found the corners of his mouth twitching. Chocky was more right than he knew, because, this time, Susie really *had* gone. She had found what she wanted, and she was content. She wouldn't come back. She'd never need to.

"Come on," he said, scratching Chocky's beak with a fingertip. "Let's get you safe in your cage and out of here!"

The mynah bird put his head on one side in his old way, the way that was reassuringly familiar.

"Chocky biscuit?" he asked hopefully.